Summer Days, Starry Nights

by Vikki VanSickle

Scholastic Canada Ltd.

Toronto New York London Auckland Sydney
Mexico City New Delhi Hong Kong Buenos Aires

Scholastic Canada Ltd.
604 King Street West, Toronto, Ontario M5V 1E1, Canada

Scholastic Inc.
557 Broadway, New York, NY 10012, USA

Scholastic Australia Pty Limited
PO Box 579, Gosford, NSW 2250, Australia

Scholastic New Zealand Limited
Private Bag 94407, Botany, Manukau 2163, New Zealand

Scholastic Children's Books
Euston House, 24 Eversholt Street, London NW1 1DB, UK

www.scholastic.ca

Library and Archives Canada Cataloguing in Publication

VanSickle, Vikki, 1982-
Summer days, starry nights / by Vikki VanSickle.
Issued also in an electronic format.
ISBN 978-1-4431-1991-7
I. Title.
PS8643.A59S86 2013   jC813'.6   C2012-907855-7

6 5 4 3 2 1   Printed in Canada 121   13 14 15 16 17

MIX
Paper from
responsible sources
FSC
www.fsc.org   FSC® C004071

PROLOGUE

I've spent enough time around campfires to know that sometimes the fire doesn't take right away. Maybe the logs are too thick or the wood too damp. Maybe a sharp wind keeps killing your flame. Whatever the reason, it can take a long time for the embers to get hot enough for the kindling to catch fire. The next thing you know, the fire is roaring away — the bark burning off the logs in black, curling strips, and the logs crumbling to a pile of white and black ash.

As a family, we Starrs had been smouldering away long before Gwendolyn Cates showed up the summer of 1962. She dropped in on us like a rag soaked in gasoline, and the sparks that had always been there, biding their time among the coals, flared up and set everything ablaze.

PART ONE
KINDLING

Summer 1961

Scarlett's Discovery

I felt the footsteps before I heard them: little wet feet slapping against the weathered planks of the dock, shaking me out of my reverie. I groaned to myself, knowing that now that my secret place had been found out, it would be secret no more.

In the past few weeks the old dock had become my home base — a place away from Scarlett's whining, from Bo and his mean comments, but mostly away from the lodge, where Mimi's disappointment hung over everything like fog. It was where I spent my free time: reading, fishing and sunning myself. I let the sunshine burn away my worries, and when I got too hot, I slipped into the lake to cool off. I was getting to be quite the angler, bringing my catch of sunfish and small bass back to Elsa to clean and prepare. Fish you catch yourself always taste better.

But fishing was about luck, and so far I hadn't had a single bite all morning. Instead, I lay flat on my back, dozing with my feet hanging off the dock. The sun was as moody as a teenager, sulking behind heavy clouds, then making brief, glaring appearances. Even the water was agitated, stirred up by a needling wind.

The feet came to a stop by my head.

"Reenie, I'm hungry," Scarlett said.

"Go tell Mimi," I muttered, not even opening my eyes.

"I can't find her."

"Did you look in the office?"

"She's not there."

"In the kitchen?"

"She's not there, either."

"Maybe she went to help Daddy."

"Daddy went into town. He was by himself; I saw him leave."

I opened my eyes and pulled myself up to rest on my elbows. "Did you check the bedroom?"

Scarlett nodded. "Yes, but she's not there."

"She must be checking on a cottage," I said, even though that was unlikely. It was Monday morning; all the cottages were full of new guests that had driven up over the weekend. Saturday was the day we cleaned the cottages. "Did you check all of them?"

Scarlett hesitated. "Not all of them," she admitted.

"Well, then. She's probably in the one you didn't check."

Scarlett wandered off again.

I tried to settle back down and find that drowsy, lazy place I had been dozing in before she'd interrupted, but the sun had vanished as quickly as it had appeared, clouds darkening the afternoon, and thoughts of Mimi darkening my mood.

When my brother Bo was little, he'd started calling our mother Mimi instead of Mama. She'd loved it, adopting the name instead of Mom, because "Mom makes me feel old."

I've never called her anything else, and neither has Bo or our little sister, Scarlett.

I can't imagine calling her Mom or Mommy, but when she laughs or greets visitors at the check-in desk, I can picture her on stage. "Your mother always wanted to be a star," Daddy liked to say. "That's why she married me."

He meant a star like in the movies, not Mrs. Dorothy Starr, his wife. It's a Starr family joke, although sometimes it feels too true to be funny.

Lately Mimi had lost a bit of her starry sheen, lapsing instead into long, dark silences. Last night at dinner she'd sat mutely at the table, staring at her food, as if she were trying to remember what to do with it. Bo and Daddy had tried to prod a response out of her by telling the kind of off-colour jokes she normally frowned upon. But after a while they gave up and continued on as if nothing were wrong. Scarlett couldn't bear it. Even though she's five years old, she'd started sucking her thumb and peppered Mimi with question after question, like a toddler. Mimi didn't seem to notice until Scarlett slid from her seat and went to sit on her lap. Mimi pet Scarlett's hair absently for a while, then stood up and muttered something about a headache. She went upstairs and shut herself in her room for the rest of the evening.

Like so many other times, Daddy had picked Scarlett up, given her a squeeze and run through every excuse he could think of: Mimi's tired, she has a headache, she isn't herself right now. But there were only so many times you could hear an excuse before it started to feel flimsy.

As the sky grew even darker, I sighed and figured that I should go see where Mimi was. As I made my way down the dock, up the dunes, across the street and toward the lodge, raindrops as big and hard as marbles fell from the sky.

Sandy Shores isn't the fanciest summer resort around, but I can't imagine another place as beautiful. My grandfather bought the land and built the lodge in 1898. By the time he died in 1944, Sandy Shores had grown to include five rental cottages. By 1960, we were up to nine cottages, a playground, four rental boats and the nicest beach on the lake.

On rainy days, most guests would hole up in their cottages, reading or napping the afternoon away. Sometimes they'd come to the dining hall to order drinks, sit around the radio and play cards until the sky cleared. And that's where I found Scarlett, sitting at the bar, stabbing maraschino cherries with a little plastic sword meant for the fancy drinks served at cocktail hour.

"What are you doing?" I demanded, as Scarlett slid a row of four sticky cherries into her mouth at once.

"I told you, I'm hungry," Scarlett said, cheeks puffing out like a chipmunk.

"Those are for the drinks," I said, whisking the jar away from her. "Not for lunch."

"I didn't know what else to eat," she whimpered.

"Come on," I sighed. "I'll make you a sandwich."

The kitchen was steamy and smelled delicious and, sure enough, when I peeked into the oven, I saw a large cut of beef roasting in its own juices. My stomach started to rumble. I was rooting through the cupboards, looking for bread, when a pair of warm, sweaty hands grabbed me lightly at the scruff of the neck.

"Aha! Mystery solved!" Elsa said. "Here I was thinking we had mice, but no, we have little girls stealing from my pantry!"

I laughed. Elsa had been at Sandy Shores ever since Daddy was a boy. Grandpa Starr had kept her on during the war, even though she was a German.

"Elsa is a Canadian who just happened to be born in Germany," Daddy explained.

She was a big woman with an even bigger voice, but I knew she was as soft as the pastries she made, before she slid them in the oven to bake. Her hair, white as the flour she baked with, was swept back in an elegant bun, and her cheeks were rosy from working over a hot stove.

"What's this," she asked, dropping her grasp on our necks to take Scarlett's messy chin in her hand. "Is *kleine* wearing lipstick already?"

Scarlett giggled and licked the sticky red syrup from her lips. "No, it's from the cherries!"

"Cherries? For lunch?" Elsa said. "It's a wonder your teeth don't fall out!"

"We're just looking for bread," I explained. "Then we'll be out of your hair."

"How can such sweet children be in my hair?" Elsa said, pinching my cheek between her thumb and forefinger. "Besides, I wear the hairnet!" Elsa snapped the elastic of her hairnet against her forehead and laughed her big, jolly, Santa-sized laugh. I rolled my eyes.

"Elsa, have you seen Mimi?" Scarlett asked, digging a knife into a jar of peanut butter.

"No, *kleine*, I have not. Perhaps she is with your father."

I gave Scarlett a hard look. "Are you *sure* she wasn't in the car?"

"I don't know, maybe," Scarlett said, but she didn't look convinced.

"Now, get!" Elsa said, shooing us toward the kitchen door. "I have dinner to prepare and those men playing cards are going to want sandwiches soon, you wait and see if I'm wrong."

"You're never wrong, Elsa," I said with a grin, grabbing a

loaf of bread and a handful of oatmeal cookies on the way out.

Scarlett and I ate peanut butter sandwiches and oatmeal cookies for lunch, washed down with tall glasses of milk that Elsa brought out for us. The rain was coming down in sheets so thick we could barely see the lake. It was cozy and smelled like roast beef in the dining hall, so we found a table in the corner, far away from the card players and their cigarettes, and I taught Scarlett to play Old Maid and Rummy until she got tired, curled up in her chair and fell asleep.

Around three, the servers started to arrive. I waved to Matthew and James in their crisp white shirts and black slacks, noting that it had been ages since I'd seen Fred or any of the other servers. I wondered if they'd been let go, and if that was why Mimi was so sad. It had been her idea to turn our modest dining hall into a proper restaurant this summer. She'd hoped to not only impress our guests, but draw in locals and passersby for the kind of fancy dinners she remembered from the city. She was always thinking of ways to give Sandy Shores a touch of sophistication, to scrub us up for our big-city guests. Before she'd met my father, Mimi had lived in the city, hoping to make it as an actress. She'd done a little modelling and was a chorus girl once, but it was wartime and there wasn't very much work. So she'd ended up pulling on a pair of overalls and working at a factory, like so many other girls, just to pay the rent. Then she met my father, fell in love and the rest is Sandy Shores history.

Sadly, the restaurant wasn't taking off like Mimi had hoped. At first she'd buzzed about, planning menus with Elsa, picking out new dishware and laughing while she folded napkins into complicated shapes every afternoon. She flirted with the serving staff, complimenting their uniforms, and she even stood behind the bar and helped mix drinks on occasion. But the crowds never really grew, and in a few weeks she went from greeting the dinner guests every evening in her best dresses, to hiding out in her bedroom during the supper hour.

"You have to give it time, Dorrie," Daddy had said, but she'd just stared at him like he was a stranger, her eyes as flat as coins. Looking around the room now, empty save for Scarlett and me and the card players, I had to admit that the whole thing had been a bust. A dining hall was one thing: it was a place for people to get a quick bite when they were too hot or tired to cook. But a fancy restaurant, with servers in cummerbunds and menu items Scarlett couldn't pronounce, was too much.

I thought Sandy Shores was as close to perfect as it could be. Why couldn't Mimi see that?

MiSSing Mimi

Scarlett and I waited for hours for Daddy to get back from town. Supper had been served and the staff was cleaning up when a pair of headlights shone through the dark like watery moons.

"They're home!" Scarlett cried, and she bolted up and ran to meet them.

But only Daddy entered the dining hall, his shirt plastered to his skin, Scarlett clinging to his arm, wailing. "She's not here, I told you, she's not here!"

Daddy pried Scarlett off his arm and hugged her to his chest. "Where's Mimi?" he asked me.

For the first time since Scarlett had asked me that hours before, I was truly worried.

"We thought she was with you," I said.

"I told you he was alone. I told you, but you didn't believe me!" Scarlett's face was a mess, red and splotchy with tears wobbling on the end of her nose and eyelashes.

"Shh, sweet pea, calm down," Daddy stroked her hair and pressed her cheek to his shoulder. Her whole body shuddered in his arms. "I'm sure she's around here somewhere."

The sound of Scarlett's wailing brought Elsa bustling into the dining hall. She clucked her tongue and gathered Scarlett into her big, soft arms, whispering sweet things to her in German.

"You're cold, *kleine*. Let Elsa warm you up some milk."

Elsa hurried back to the kitchen, cuddling Scarlett.

Daddy looked at me. "When did you see her last?"

I had to think about it. Mimi had been such a ghost lately, floating through life with as few words as possible, that I couldn't remember. It seemed ages since I had had any real contact with her.

Daddy slammed his fist against the bar. The sound brought tears to my eyes. When he spoke, it wasn't anger in his voice, it was fear. Anger would have been less scary.

"Think, Reenie, when did you see her last?"

"Last night, after dinner," I whispered. I didn't mention that she had been lying on her bed, unable or unwilling to even lift her head when I'd brought in a plate of food.

Daddy looked grim. I saw lines in his face that I hadn't noticed before. His cheeks sagged like an old man's. It was as if I had caught a glimpse of him twenty years in the future, and I didn't like what I saw. He sighed and ran his hands through his wet hair, slicking it back against his scalp.

"I'm going to make some phone calls. Where's Bo?"

Tears made their way down my cheeks. I couldn't hold them in anymore.

"I don't know," I admitted, hot with shame. What kind of person was I? I didn't know where my mother or brother was.

"You look after Scarlett," Daddy said, then he turned on his heel and stalked off.

I found Scarlett on Elsa's lap. There was flour in her hair where Elsa's kind hands had been stroking it. Even though it was hot and sticky in the kitchen, Scarlett was shivering violently. Elsa had draped an old lumpy sweater over Scarlett's thin shoulders. Her little white hands were wrapped around a mug, and she kept staring into the curls of steam that rose to her face.

Elsa looked up and smiled sadly at me. She nodded toward the stove, where a shallow pan of milk was simmering. I ladled us two mugs of hot milk, stirring in heaping spoons of Ovaltine. We stared at our hot chocolate in silence, Elsa humming and Scarlett whimpering. Eventually Scarlett cried herself out and began to droop against Elsa's bosom.

"I think you should take her up to bed," Elsa said softly.

"But Mimi—" Scarlett was overcome with a yawn before she could finish her sentence.

"Come on," I said, shifting her weight from Elsa to my own arms.

Like a toddler, Scarlett wrapped her arms around my neck and let herself be lifted. I staggered under the weight of her. She was getting too big to be carried around like a baby, especially by a twelve-year-old like me, even though I was strong from years of tree-climbing and arm wrestling with Bo.

We lived on the second floor of the lodge, except for Bo. This summer he had moved into the attic room so he could play his guitar at any hour of the day without disturbing anyone. We rarely rented rooms on the second floor, but when we did, we tended to rent the ones on the west end of the lodge so we could maintain our privacy.

I loved the lodge, but it felt eerie being upstairs, just the two of us, alone in the dark, knowing Mimi and maybe even Bo were out there somewhere in the rain.

The window had been left open in Scarlett's room, and the dampness had crept in and settled over everything. I let

Scarlett down on the bed as gently as I could, the muscles in my arms shaking with the effort.

"I'm not sleepy," Scarlett insisted, but she nuzzled her head against the pillow anyway.

"Just close your eyes," I suggested, tucking her ragged teddy Boo-Bear in beside her. "You don't have to sleep yet."

"Will you stay with me?"

Scarlett's voice sounded small in the darkness. I reached out and felt her cheek, cool and clammy from all the tears she had cried. I perched carefully on the edge of her bed, letting my shoes drop to the floor.

"All the way in," Scarlett insisted. The storm was still pouring rain outside the window. I leaned back against her pillow, and I watched the shadowy patterns of the branches just outside the window dance across the ceiling in the lights from the patio. Scarlett's cold little feet pressed into my shins but I didn't want to move her. She seemed so comfortable. We lay like that, listening to the rain clatter against the window, until Scarlett's hiccupping stopped and she began to breathe evenly. I was relieved and a little jealous at the ease Scarlett had falling to sleep, given the circumstances. My heart was racing, and despite being bone-tired, I knew I wouldn't sleep much this evening.

I couldn't stop thinking about the restaurant and how it had failed, seeming to suck the life from Mimi. She took things harder than most people, suffering from dark moods that kept her locked away for days at a time.

Daddy had been unsure of her plan from the beginning. He'd said the kind of restaurant Mimi had in mind was too grand for the area, and no one wanted to eat a three-course meal in a building with an exposed timber frame and sand between the floorboards. But Mimi had insisted. "A little class never hurt anybody," she'd said. Then, narrowing her eyes at Daddy, "It wouldn't hurt you to dress up for dinner once in a while. You look like a fisherman."

I remember Daddy laughing. "No one in their right mind is going to be looking at me when they could be looking at you," he'd said. "Besides, I think I look like a man who runs a resort. People see these boots and these work clothes and think, 'Now there's a man who knows what he's doing.' A man in a cummerbund and bowtie isn't likely to help you bring your boat in, now is he?"

Daddy had leaned in and given Mimi a quick peck on the cheek, being extra careful not to brush against her good dress in his dusty old work shirt, yellowed around the collar and smelling of lake water and sweat. "You're the face and I'm the muscle," he'd said.

Mimi had smiled, taking one of Daddy's rough, dirty hands between her own, which were clean, white and perfectly manicured. "So who's the brains?" she'd asked, a twinkle in her eye.

Daddy had winked at me. "Reenie, of course."

My heart had soared, and I'd wondered if he meant it, or if he was just buttering me up, like one of our guests.

He knew I loved Sandy Shores with all my heart. I couldn't imagine living anywhere else. Sometimes Bo talked about how great it would be to travel the country on a bus with his band, doing a show in a different town every night. When he got on that train of thought, it was best just to let him go on until he'd talked himself out. He was more stubborn than a bird with a worm, and when Bo decided something was so, there was no use arguing. But the truth was, I'd take the lake and a pair of white sand dunes over a stage and a tour bus any day.

* * *

A door slammed and I sat straight up in bed. I glanced at Scarlett, but she was sound asleep. I inched out of bed and silently flew out the door. A razor-thin blade of light shone under the office door. I knocked softly and went in. Daddy was slumped in the chair, the phone in his hand. I could hear the dial tone from where I was standing. Bo was standing by the doorway, rain pooled on the brim of his hat.

"Where's Scarlett?" Daddy asked.

"Asleep." I looked at Bo. "Where have you been?"

"Out searching."

"Any luck?"

Bo shook his head, sending rain flying in every direction.

"Maybe she's on a bus. Or a train," I suggested.

"A train going where?" Bo said.

I shrugged, miserable. "Maybe she had a doctor's appointment she forgot about."

Daddy shook his head. "There's nothing on the calendar."

"Maybe she forgot to write it down, and they called and she left in a hurry."

Daddy sighed. "That may be, Reenie, but where is she now? It's ten thirty at night."

"Maybe she missed her bus. And the storm knocked down the telephone lines and she can't call. She probably had to stay in town for the night."

"I called all the hotels in Orillia."

"Maybe she stayed with someone in town, a friend."

Bo frowned, and I looked away. We both knew Mimi had no friends in Orillia, not real ones. She often lamented the lack of eligible companions out here "in the boonies." Maybe if she had more friends she would be here right now.

"I'm just trying to help," I said weakly.

17

Daddy sighed. "I know that. You're a good girl, Maureen."

An idea flashed in my brain. "Did she leave a note?"

Daddy turned ashen. "A note?" he repeated.

"You know, telling us where she was going."

Bo hung his hat on the hook by the door and headed for the stairs, grabbing my elbow along the way. "Come on, it's late."

"But Mimi—"

Bo whispered in my ear. "Let it alone, Reenie."

I wished Daddy good night and followed Bo upstairs, worried about Daddy, scared for Mimi and mad at Bo for treating me like I was stupid. Once we were on the second floor and out of earshot, Bo spun me around by my elbow and hissed, "Don't you know when to say when? Don't you think he's had a hard enough day as it is?"

I tore my elbow from his grasp and rubbed it. "It's a reasonable question — did she leave a note?"

"Come on, Reenie, use your brain! Even you can't be that slow."

"I don't understand."

Bo looked over his shoulder, as if expecting to see someone, but the hallway was empty. His next words left me cold. "Suicides leave notes."

I opened my mouth to protest, but only a squeak came out. When I was able to speak, words rushed out of me like blood from a wound.

"You're the one who doesn't know when to say when! Mimi would never do anything like that! She loves us! Women with three children don't just up and kill themselves."

Bo looked at me sadly. "Women with three children don't just get up and go, leaving their families behind, either."

I watched him climb the stairs to his attic kingdom, abandoning me with a head full of dark thoughts.

The Mimi Hunt

In the morning, I woke with a kink in my neck and pins and needles up and down my left arm, which Scarlett had rolled over and taken possession of in the night. She hugged it to her chest fiercely, like a teddy bear. I slipped from her grasp, one careful inch at a time.

Outside, it was bright and sunny; a perfect summer day. Last night's rain had washed away all the dust, and everything looked so freshly scrubbed, I wouldn't have been surprised to reach out and find that the leaves squeaked between my fingers. Already I could hear laughter and the slap of screen doors as people headed down to the beach for the day. It felt wrong. How could it be such a beautiful day when everything was falling apart?

Eventually, the smell of bacon got to Scarlett, and she sat up, bleary-eyed and rubbing her stomach.

"Is Mimi back?" she asked.

"I don't know," I admitted. "I only just got up."

Scarlett brightened. "Maybe she's downstairs!" she said, throwing on some clothes, then running ahead of me toward the dining hall, taking the stairs two at a time.

But all we found when we got there was Elsa, frying strip bacon in a pan. Scarlett ran to the office, then up to Mimi and Daddy's bedroom, only to return looking disappointed. But at least she didn't cry. I doubted she could if she'd wanted to, having wrung herself dry of any tears last night.

Elsa cracked two eggs in the pan above a piece of sputtering bacon, making a smiley face just for Scarlett. She sang songs and tickled her sides, but Scarlett remained a sober version of herself.

After, I shooed Scarlett upstairs to wash up, and I went to talk to Daddy in the office. He looked up as I walked in, his whole face tensed and hopeful. Then his shoulders dropped, and I could tell by his sad smile that he'd hoped I was Mimi.

He did his best to hide this by coming over, kissing the top of my head and wrapping me in a bear hug so tight, he squeezed the breath right out of me.

"I can't breathe!"

Daddy released me and stepped back, ruffling my hair. "Sorry."

I hated to wreck the moment, but I had to ask. "Well?"

"Nothing yet."

My breakfast rumbled in my stomach, threatening to make a surprise appearance all over the desk.

"I'd appreciate it if you looked after Scarlett today."

"What should I tell her?"

Daddy sighed the kind of world-weary sigh I associated with Mimi, but not with him. "Tell her she's on a shopping trip."

"A shopping trip?" I repeated.

Daddy shrugged. "Maybe she is."

"But what are we going to do when she shows up here without any shopping bags?"

"We don't know that she won't."

I didn't know what else to say. It was clear by the set of his chin and the calm in his eyes that he believed it. In that moment he reminded me of Scarlett. Beautiful, sunny Scarlett, whom everyone always thought of as Mimi's child. She may have had Mimi's colouring and glamour, but Scarlett had inherited Daddy's disposition — an unshakable faith in others that worried me.

"Just keep her distracted, would you, Reenie? I'll get the serving staff to take shifts in the office," he said.

"I'll try," I agreed, though secretly I had no idea how I was going to keep a five-year-old from thinking about her missing mother.

It turned out I had no reason to be worried. Sometime between breakfast and getting washed up, Scarlett had decided that she was going to find Mimi herself. She emerged from her bedroom with one of Mimi's old purses slung over her shoulder.

"What's in that?" I asked.

"Supplies," she explained, clicking open the clasp to show me her collection. "I'm going on a Mimi hunt."

The purse bulged with pencils, ribbons, a notepad, a plastic toy compass that had come as a gift in a cereal box, an old whistle on a red string and a fat romance novel.

"What's the book for?"

"It's Mimi's. I took it from her nightstand. She hasn't finished it. I thought it would remind her that she still has things to do here."

I dropped to my knees and hugged Scarlett just as Daddy had hugged me, so she would know she was loved. When she had had enough, she squirmed in my arms and muttered, "Ouch," in my ear.

I let her go, blowing the bangs from her eyes, and said, "What a great idea."

I took the book from Scarlett's purse. It looked like every other romance novel. On the cover, a woman swooned in the arms of a handsome man. They both had faces drawn in lusty expressions that made me blush. Mimi had stuck a nail file between the pages as a bookmark. I opened the book to where she had left off and started to read: *Jeanette could bear it no longer. The days were endless and offered no comfort without David's warm embrace. "If I stay here, I will die," she thought.*

I closed the book and shoved it back into the purse.

"What's it about?" Scarlett asked.

"Nothing," I said. "Just another silly romance novel with lots of kissing." I made smacking noises with my lips, trying to cheer her up.

Scarlett wrinkled her nose. "Yech! Are you coming with me?"

"Of course," I said. "Just let me get some more supplies."

Scarlett rattled her purse, frowning. "I have everything here," she insisted.

"I was thinking more along the lines of sandwiches and lemonade, and maybe hats."

"Okay," Scarlett agreed. "But hurry."

* * *

I spent all morning and the better part of the afternoon trailing behind Scarlett as she marched around Sandy Shores looking for Mimi. We looked under cottages, behind the fish hut, in the trees and even in the boathouse, which was usually avoided at all costs. Bo had once told Scarlett a wild story about monster rats living in the rafters.

To be fair, he'd done it to keep her from wandering in there when she was alone, and it could be a dangerous place. But Scarlett's determination to find Mimi trumped her fear of two-headed, man-eating rats, and we searched every inch of the boathouse, Scarlett gripping my hand the whole time.

On a beautiful day like this, most of the boats were out on the lake, or tied up at the docks, but three motorboats were housed in the building.

"Search every one," Scarlett insisted.

The play of shadows against the wall and the sound of the waves slapping against the boats set me on edge, but I peeled back the tarps on all three, squinting into their dark bellies, for Scarlett's sake. We found nothing but old lures, waterlogged maps and tangles of fishing line, which looked like old spider webs.

Before we left, Scarlett tied an old yellow hair ribbon to the door handle. "That way we know we've been here," she explained.

My job was to take notes. I recorded our every step, along with anything that might be a clue. Down the road, near the bluffs, Scarlett found a suspiciously thinned patch of Queen Anne's lace, the gauzy blossoms nodding in the breeze.

"Flowers have been picked here recently!" she cried. "It's a clue! Write it down!"

In the playground, we found a child's shovel, five marbles and a pair of cracked sunglasses. I recorded them in the notebook as Scarlett collected them and put them gently in her purse. She paused to examine the sunglasses, oversized with white frames, dirty from being buried in the sand.

"They aren't Mimi's," I said softly.

Scarlett turned on me, rage crossing her face like a storm

cloud. "You don't know that. You don't know anything."

I didn't scold her, I didn't even contradict her. I just nod-ded and wrote, *Sunglasses, white, by the slide in the play-ground.* Scarlett tied one ribbon to a metal link in the chain of the swing set and one to the stem of a particularly tall dandelion.

"Are you hungry? Do you want a sandwich?" I asked.

Scarlett shook her head. "Detectives don't get hungry," she said.

* * *

That night, Scarlett took the marbles she had found in the playground and put them in a dish on her nightstand. She had washed them in soapy water until they shone as good as new, leaving a gritty ring of sand on the white enamel of the bathroom sink.

"What are those for?" I asked.

"Luck," she said. "Five marbles for five Starrs."

Then she picked them up, one by one, and bid them each good night with a kiss before settling them back in the dish.

"Good night, Daddy; good night, Bo; good night, Reenie; good night, Scarlett; good night, Mimi, wherever you are."

Five Marbles for Five Starrs

After two days, it became clear that the Mimi hunt was a bust. Scarlett's optimism began to flicker, and I was desperate to do whatever I could to keep its flame alive. She followed me around like a little rain cloud, gloomy and sad. And so I did whatever I could to distract her. I took her fishing, and we collected flowers to make bouquets for all the tables in the dining hall. I even taught her to climb the Lookout, my favourite tree. It dominated our front lawn, and if you went up far enough, you could see for miles around. Scarlett took to climbing like it was something she had been born doing, without a lick of fear or hesitation. But best of all, I knew Mimi wouldn't approve. It felt like a small victory, teaching her to do something that Mimi wouldn't like. If she was so worried about us, then where was she?

One night, I spied three figures silhouetted in the window of the office. Daddy, Bo and someone else: someone tall, wearing a hat. I peered around the lodge and saw a police car parked on the grass. My stomach lurched.

25

"Scarlett, you go on up and get your PJs on. I'll be there in a second."

"I want to see Daddy."

"No!" I practically shouted it.

"Why not?"

"Because he's busy. He'll come up later."

I must have sounded serious, either that or Scarlett was too tired to argue, because she pushed open the screen door and made her way up the stairs. I followed her in, but turned and headed in the opposite direction, toward the office. The door was shut, but voices drifted into the hallway. They were low, but they didn't sound angry or sad. Daddy answered on the first knock, but no one opened the door.

"Yes?"

"It's Reenie. Can I come in?"

The door swung open and I blinked in the light. Bo was leaning against the desk and Daddy was showing the police chief, Chief Bowen, his fishing rod. Chief Bowen touched the brim of his hat and smiled at me. My heart felt like it was clenched inside a cruel fist. He was wearing his police hat, which meant this was an official visit, despite the casual way he was smiling at me.

"Good evening, Reenie. You're getting tall."

I couldn't be bothered with manners. "What are you doing here?" I asked. "Where's my mother?"

"Reenie, go on up to bed. We're just talking through the events with Chief Bowen here. There's nothing to worry about," Daddy said.

Wrong, I thought. There is everything to worry about. "But I—"

"I'll come up later when we're done and kiss you good night."

I had said practically the same thing to Scarlett minutes before. I blushed, embarrassed to be treated like a five-year-old in front of the police chief.

I made my way upstairs and fell into bed without even brushing my teeth or washing my face. I stepped out of my shorts but left my shirt on. I couldn't be bothered with PJs. Scarlett came in from the bathroom smelling like toothpaste and trees and joined me in the bed, wrapping herself around one arm and resting her chin on my shoulder. It was too hot to be that close, but I didn't have the heart to pry her off.

"Kiss the marbles," she murmured in my ear.

I picked up the marbles and kissed each one, whispering, "Good night Daddy; good night Bo; good night Reenie; good night Scarlett; good night Mimi, wherever you are."

Within minutes Scarlett fell asleep, leaving me lying awake with nothing to do but think. Daddy says too much thinking is bad for a person, and that it's just as important to get out and do things. Maybe that was Mimi's problem. Too much thinking had poisoned her mind and now she had gone and done something crazy. And what about me? Surely talking things over with me was better than leaving me alone in the dark thinking about them?

Downstairs, I heard a door click closed, and then a car started and rumbled into the night. Chief Bowen had left. I could still hear Daddy and Bo in the office. They were having one of their secret, grown-up meetings that I wasn't invited to. Daddy said it was because someone had to stay with Scarlett, but I knew it was because he thought I was too young for such conversations. That stung almost as much as Bo's stupid, thoughtless comments about Mimi. I spent all day entertaining Scarlett and all night sleeping beside her in case she woke up crying, or needed a glass of water. I made sure she got enough sun and fresh air so that she was tuckered out by nightfall and slept soundly, even without Mimi to tuck her in. Hadn't I earned a place in important family discussions?

I heard footsteps on the stairs. Bo, or Daddy? They came to a stop outside the door. Definitely Daddy. I rolled over and pretended to be asleep.

"You awake, Reenie?" he whispered.

I made my breathing slow and even, so he would think I was sleeping. I couldn't see him with my eyes closed, but he must have stood there for a while, silent as an owl, because I was half asleep for real when I heard him whisper, "Good night."

* * *

On Sunday I woke up dry-mouthed, hot and sticky and unsure of where I was. Then I rolled over and saw Scarlett and remembered that I was sleeping in her room. And then I remembered why.

I lay in bed listening to the birds outside the window until Scarlett stirred. Then I followed her as she raced down the stairs and into the kitchen. I worried about how I was going to distract her today.

Only this time, Mimi was there waiting for us.

Scarlett and I stopped dead in our tracks, stumbling into the dining room as the door swung back and hit us both from behind. It was just like I had imagined, only I had stopped believing it would actually happen. I resisted the urge to rub my eyes, in case I blinked and she disappeared.

Mimi was sitting at the bar with Daddy, both of them holding thick white mugs of coffee. Her lavender dressing gown was cinched around her waist. Her hair was set in rollers all over her head, like the interlocking cells of a honeycomb. Her face was pale, but I could tell instantly that she was regular Mimi, not the black mood that took hold of her and drained her of all the good things that made her Mimi. She smiled brightly at us, stood up and opened her arms.

Scarlett was the first to snap out of the dumb shock that had frozen us in place, and she threw herself against Mimi. It took me a bit longer to thaw. I hung back as Mimi tucked Scarlett's hair behind her ears and covered her cheeks with glossy kisses.

"When did you get back?" Scarlett demanded.

"Last night."

"Why you didn't wake me up?"

"It was very late," Mimi said.

I looked over at Daddy to see if it was true. He looked a little sheepish. "We came in to check on you, and you were both fast asleep," he explained.

How could I have slept through my mother's return, and not known that she had crept in to check on us in the night? That seemed like the sort of thing a person should sense.

"Did you miss us?" Scarlett asked.

"Every single day."

"You were gone for a long time."

"I know," Mimi said. "But I'm back now."

"For good?" Scarlett asked, putting a hand on either side of Mimi's cheeks and staring her directly in the face.

Mimi looked very solemn. She placed her own hands on top of Scarlett's before replying, "Yes, for good."

"Wait until you see the loot your mother picked up for you girls," Daddy said, whistling.

"Presents?" Scarlett cried. "Where?"

Mimi laughed. "You'll have to wait until after breakfast," she said.

"Where's Bo?" I asked.

Everyone looked at me.

"Come give your mother a hug," Daddy said. "You haven't seen her in a week and the first thing you say is 'where's Bo?'"

"It's not like I asked her to go away for a week," I said evenly, avoiding Mimi's eyes. "Where's Bo?"

Mimi's smile faltered a little, but she recovered quickly, shifting Scarlett to one side and beckoning to me with her free arm. "Bo's out fishing. Come give me a hug, Maureen. I missed you so much."

I didn't want to go to her, but I did it anyway, for Scarlett and for Daddy, who so desperately wanted things to go back to normal. As if nothing had ever happened.

I leaned stiffly into Mimi and let her squeeze me and tell me how much she missed me, and I wished I was with Bo, out on the lake, away from this charade.

When Mimi brought out the presents, I paid close attention to the price tags. Everything had come from stores in Orillia. I knew that both Daddy and Bo, and probably Chief Bowen, too, had searched everywhere they could think of in Orillia. There was no way Mimi could have hidden in a town that small for a whole week. She had disappeared and returned under the cloak of night. Wherever she had been in between was still a mystery, but it sure wasn't Orillia. These presents had been chosen and paid for by Daddy. The knowledge made me feel old and slightly sad, like I had learned the truth about Santa Claus all over again.

For the rest of the summer, Scarlett and I went back to living fairly separate lives. I was surprised to find how much

I missed her. Even though I relished my freedom, I felt a little betrayed. For a whole week I had been Scarlett's playmate and protector, and she dropped me without a thought the second Mimi returned.

We never spoke of Mimi's disappearance again, at least not to each other. Everyone went back to their old routines, but two things remained. Scarlett was a champion tree climber, scaling the Lookout to a height that even I hadn't attempted. The more Mimi begged her to come down, the higher she climbed. And secondly, the marbles remained in their dish by her bedside, inches away from Scarlett's pillow. One night, months later, I overheard Mimi asking her what those dusty marbles were doing rolling around in her good tea saucer.

"They're for luck," Scarlett said. "Five marbles for five Starrs."

"Which one is mine?" Mimi asked.

"This one."

"It has a chip in it."

"That's because you were bad. You went away without saying goodbye."

The marbles stayed where they were. Mimi never asked about them again.

PART TWO
SPARKS

June and July, 1962

A Family Meeting

"Reenie, come down from that tree. Your mother has called a family meeting."

From where I was sitting in the lap of the Lookout, I could see a bald spot on the very top of Daddy's head that I had never seen before. How could I, when our usual position was on the ground — me looking up and him looking down? He'd brushed his hair over it best he could, but it was there, like a worn elbow in an old jacket.

"Coming," I called, but I watched him head back to the lodge before making my way down. I needed time to think about that bald spot. How long had it been there, and if it wasn't for the tree and my bird's-eye view, how long would it have been before I noticed it? A bald spot seems like the kind of thing a daughter should notice.

I notice lots of things. Sandy Shores is full of secrets, if you know where to look. At first glance everything is pretty as a postcard: rustic old lodge overlooking a sandy beach white as sugar. The linens may be new and the dining hall freshly painted, but for every swept corner and trimmed bush there are shadows and sinkholes. I definitely notice more than Bo or Scarlett. But maybe that's because Bo is too busy with his guitar and Scarlett is too busy being adorable. Being in the middle makes me perfectly positioned to notice things that others don't. Like Mimi.

She had been brooding again, lost in her own thoughts. After she'd returned last summer, she was as good as gold all year: attentive, loving and full of careful laughter. But recently I had caught her staring out the window, stirring her tea absently, long after it had turned cold. She was silent at meals and once served us chocolate pudding before the meatloaf. I recognized Mimi's moods like I recognized cloud patterns, and just like the low clouds that circle before a storm, I knew something big was brewing in her head.

It made me nervous.

* * *

Our usual table, tucked into the corner of the dining hall, near the kitchen, had been set for dinner even though it was barely four o'clock. There was even a plate of roast chicken and creamed corn. Elsa had only been back for two weeks, but already I could feel my shorts getting tighter. She was a wonderful cook. Without her jams and jars of homemade preserves, I was certain the Starrs would never make it through the winter. My mother was good at a lot of things, but cooking wasn't one of them.

As I came in, Mimi smiled at me and poured me a glass of milk. "Ah, Reenie, there you are."

I slipped into my spot at the table and tucked into the food. I didn't know I was hungry until my stomach started growling. My plate was almost clean when Mimi cleared her throat.

"I've been thinking," she began, setting her cutlery aside. "Maybe what this place needs is some entertainment." She spoke as if we were in the middle of a conversation. Bo and I exchanged glances, but Daddy continued to eat as if he knew exactly what she was talking about. "The big hotels have ballrooms with dancing and a live band. I heard that Gravenhurst even has a variety show with professional singers on Tuesday evenings. We wouldn't need something that grand, at least not to start with. We could have lessons during the day and then a dance every once in a while."

Daddy spoke up, his words measured and careful. "We're only a month away from the start of the season. Where are we going to find someone to run this entertainment?" he asked.

"You don't have to worry about that, I'll take care of it."

Daddy looked up from his plate, surprised. "You would do that?"

Mimi smoothed her skirt and straightened her shoulders. "I think I'd be good at it. I used to work at a supper club, Frank. You know that."

I held my breath and kept my eyes down, hoping against hope that Daddy would say yes. He had decided to scale down the restaurant after last year's disappointment. Now we had only one server, with Bo on hand to help out if things got busy. Show biz wasn't really Daddy's thing, but it was so rare for Mimi to take an interest in anything about Sandy Shores that I was sure he couldn't refuse.

I was right. Daddy swallowed and a big old smile crept across his face. "Well, sure, Dorrie. I think that's a fine idea. Why don't you look into it a little?"

"Actually, I have an idea," Mimi paused for dramatic effect. I looked over at Daddy, who looked genuinely surprised.

"What is it?" I asked, practically on the edge of my seat.

"Not what, who," Mimi said with a smile. "Gwendolyn Cates."

"Who?" Bo mumbled.

I gasped. "How could you forget?"

Mimi frowned. "You remember Gwendolyn," she said. "She came to stay here once. My friend Grace's daughter? The ballet dancer?"

"Oh, her," Bo said, then went back to his plate.

"How come I don't remember her?" Scarlett asked.

"You were too young, sweet pea," Mimi said.

Daddy put down his fork; he looked worried. "Are you sure that's a good idea, Dorrie? We don't really know her all that well . . ."

Mimi flushed. "I think she would be a perfect fit. I'll telephone Grace and see if Gwendolyn is available."

I thought it was a great plan. The idea of Gwendolyn coming all the way from Toronto to Sandy Shores to teach dance thrilled me to my very bones. I tucked back into my baked potato, prepared just the way I like it, with big dollops of sour cream and sliced pickles. The summer was starting to look brighter every moment.

Trouble in Paradise

Neither Mimi nor Daddy had mentioned anything about Sandy Shores being in trouble, but I'd overheard them talking about it through the winter. They were worried about our numbers. We'd had fewer guests last summer than ever before.

I knew this already, because for the first time that I could remember, there were a number of weeks where one or two of our cottages were unoccupied. Though, at the time, I was too busy having fun playing in the empty cottages to realize that it meant bad news. This year, preregistration was down, and it looked like we were about to have another bad season.

The thought of Sandy Shores being in trouble made my heart ache and my stomach twist into sailor's knots. Sandy Shores was more than my home. It was in my blood, passed down through the generations like blue eyes or dimples. I wasn't sure I could live without it. The only person who loved Sandy Shores as much as I did was Daddy. He loved

Sandy Shores more than anything else in the whole world. Not more than Mimi or Bo or Scarlett or me, but pretty close. After my grandfather died, Daddy had special permission to come home from the war to take over the business.

Daddy never talks about the war, though. When pressed, usually by Bo, all he says is that he thought about home every second of every day. "Sometimes, the smell was so bad, I couldn't keep any food down. So I thought of waking up here and taking a big deep breath. Kids, I have been all over the place, and I can honestly say that we have the sweetest smelling air in the whole wide world."

I knew exactly what he meant. The air at Sandy Shores smells like a combination of lake water, campfire, grass and tanning oil. It is sweet, salty, pungent and fresh. Mimi's forever dabbing perfume behind her ears and rubbing creams into her skin to smell "more like a lady and less like a fish hut," but I love the way I smell after a day in the sun. I fall asleep at night burrowing my nose in the crook of my elbow, breathing in the smell of the lake on my skin.

"Some men dream of coming home to their sweethearts," Mimi said ruefully, "but not your father. He dreamed of coming home to the woods with all the blackflies."

I wished on every star I saw that Daddy would leave the business to me, even though I'm a girl. Who had ever heard of a girl running a resort by herself? It just wasn't done. Bo was the one who stood to take over our little piece of heaven. He was the oldest and a boy, which meant that I had two strikes against me, even though Bo always got out of his chores and would rather be in town at the movies than weeding or raking the beach.

If Sandy Shores was in trouble, then it needed me more than ever. I thought it was perfect just the way it was, but if dazzling our guests with a big show was the way to bring people in and keep us afloat, then I was on board one hundred percent.

Maybe the restaurant hadn't taken off like we'd hoped, but entertainment was something Mimi had in her bones. She was going to save us all with her dramatic flair and love of glamour. Before, it had set her apart, like she was a parrot from the jungle set free in the middle of Ontario. The rest of us, we fit in like the loons in the lake or the rabbits that lived in the woods at the edge of the property. But Mimi was too shiny, too exotic. She wouldn't last two days out here on her own. On my darkest days I wondered if that was what brought on her moods and made her so sad.

Take me away from Sandy Shores and I wouldn't survive, like a fish out of water. Take Mimi away, and she'd never look back.

A SCaRF FuLL oF
MeMORieS

A few days later, Mimi stood up at breakfast and clinked a
fork against her water glass.

.   "I have an announcement," she said.

We all looked up from our eggs, even Bo, who was having trouble keeping his eyes open. I had heard him creep
in through his window late last night for the second time
in a week. He was probably with his band again. Lately his
bandmates seemed to be the only people Bo could stand
to be around. Bo and I had never been best friends, but
we used to do things together. He taught me to jump from
the cliff and how to slit a blade of glass to make a whistle.
Now all he did was glower at me, when he could even be
bothered to look my way. I had half a mind to let Mimi and
Daddy know what he was up to, but watching him struggle
to stay awake was worth it in its own way.

Mimi went on, "I'm thrilled to say that Gwendolyn has
agreed to come and teach dance this summer."

Scarlett and I cheered. Daddy got up and kissed Mimi on the cheek.

"That's wonderful, Dorrie," he said.

Mimi beamed, dropping a hand to pet Scarlett's silky head. "Aren't we lucky? A real ballet dancer, here for the whole summer!"

I was ecstatic that Gwendolyn would be returning. It had been six years since she visited, but I had bright memories of that weekend. She had been so exotic, a ballerina in training, graceful, athletic and fun. I thought about her from time to time, and how different her life was from mine; growing up in a big city, taking lessons at a prestigious ballet school. She would be almost eighteen now. She was practically an adult. I bet she went out dancing and had lots of boyfriends. I had visions of us staying up late, giggling in bed while she told me story after story about her exciting life.

"Maybe she can stay in my room," I offered.

"Don't be silly, she'll have her own room," Mimi said.

Daddy frowned. "Take away a room from a paying customer all summer?" he said.

"She's a guest and an employee!" Mimi exclaimed. "We can't have her bunking with Reenie as if she's here for an extended sleepover!"

My cheeks burned. That was exactly what I had been imagining.

"Besides, it's not like we don't have the room," Mimi muttered. Daddy's face darkened and I got that sour milk feeling in my stomach. In all the excitement I had forgotten the reason Gwendolyn was coming in the first place. Sandy Shores was in trouble. This was a rescue mission.

"Well, I think it's great! I can't wait to see her again!" I said.

"Remember, Reenie, she's here to work," Mimi cautioned.

"Yeah," Bo chimed in. "She won't have time to babysit."

"I don't need a babysitter!" I cried.

"Are you sure? 'Cause you're sure acting like a baby, Weenie!"

Bo grinned, got up and darted for the kitchen, laughing. His drowsiness had burned off and he was back to his usual self. I had long since given up trying to chase him. His legs were just that much longer and he was just that much faster than I was.

"Please don't pout, Maureen. It isn't ladylike."

I tried to shake it off, but no matter how I tried, Bo always got to me. I was certain Gwendolyn would never do such a thing.

* * *

Before bed that night I went down to the kitchen to get a glass of milk. On my way back I noticed a light in the dining hall. It was late and we didn't have any guests yet, so I went to investigate. I found Mimi, sitting by the windows, her feet tucked under her. She was hunched over something.

"Mimi?"

She looked up sharply, then smiled. "Reenie. What are you doing up?"

"I wanted a glass of milk."

"Come here, sweet pea."

She hadn't called me that in ages. I flushed with pleasure and padded over, happy to have a moment alone with her. As I got closer, I saw an old silk scarf on her lap and a jumble of familiar objects in front of her on the table.

"What are you doing?" I asked, even though I knew.

"Remembering," Mimi said with a sigh. She patted the chair beside her. "Come here."

I knew these objects. They belonged to Mimi's past. When I was little I used to love sitting with her and hearing all about her life, before Daddy and before us. It sounded so glamorous, like something out of a book, but here were the objects to prove it. There were notes and cards, mostly from friends, but a few from admirers. Like the playbill she kept as a memento of a date with a much older man.

"A theatre producer," she confided.

"What was it like?" I asked, clutching the playbill, hungry for romantic details, like candlelit dinners and dancing across marbled ballroom floors.

But Mimi misunderstood my question. "It was mediocre at best," she sniffed, meaning the play. "The lead slurred his lines and the nicest thing any of the critics could say about the leading lady was what a knockout she was."

I fished through the pile on Mimi's lap, looking for my favourite objects: a slim brass key, an old locket, and a photograph of my mother, taken when she was eighteen.

The key was from Mimi's first apartment. "It was just a room in a rooming house for girls, not really an apartment at all," Mimi admitted. "About six of us shared a bathroom that was so cold I felt like I was back home in the outhouse every time I needed to use the toilet. We used to hang our towels over the radiators in our rooms to keep them nice and toasty so at the very least you could step out of an ice-cold shower into a warm towel. But it was the first place where I was on my own. I could lounge in bed all day or eat eggs at two o'clock in the morning and no one could stop me."

The locket had a broken clasp and was not very grand. Being tied up in a scarf all these years had taken the sheen off the silver, which was now cloudy looking and felt greasy beneath my fingers. Inside, a loop of light hair was braided and curled. It was pale and wispy, like Scarlett's hair. Or maybe it was a lock of Mimi's baby hair. I took the loop of hair out to get a closer look.

"Don't touch that!" Mimi said sharply, rapping me on the wrist.

Ashamed, I set the loop of hair back into the locket as gently as possible and clicked it shut, as if I were tucking it into bed. I was too flustered to ask about the hair and which of us it belonged to. I didn't want to risk being scolded again.

The photograph featured my mother and her best friend, Grace. Gwendolyn's mother. I studied it carefully. In the photograph, they are posing in front of a busy outdoor rink, bundled up against the cold in sweaters and scarves. They look like sisters, with their light hair curling under their fuzzy hats. Mimi stares right into the camera, smiling with all the charm of a movie star. Grace is holding onto my mother's arm with both hands, looking both delighted and afraid.

"Grace had never been skating before," Mimi remembered, shaking her head. "Can you imagine?"

I couldn't. All the Starrs learned to skate almost as soon as they could walk. Daddy would clear a patch of ice near the beach every winter, and we'd spend Sunday afternoons learning our cross-cuts and playing ice tag.

Grace and my mother rarely saw each other after Mimi moved up here, but Grace still sent a Christmas letter every December, detailing the events of the year and filling us in on her life. I couldn't have cared less about the prices at Eaton's or what kind of car the neighbours bought, but I loved to hear about Gwendolyn. And to think — soon she would be here, at Sandy Shores!

I thought of Mimi's keepsakes — the key, locket and

photograph — as clues to her past. On more than one occasion I'd spied her in her room, on the bed, the scarf sitting open in her lap, crying silently to herself. I never asked her what was wrong, because I was afraid of the answer.

"Mimi?"

"Mmm?"

"I'm glad that Gwendolyn is coming this summer."

"Me, too."

"It'll be nice to have another girl around," I said. "Show Bo he's not the king."

Mimi laughed softly — a little sadly, I thought — and kissed the top of my head.

"It'll be nice for all of us."

I finished my milk and left Mimi in the dining hall, remembering. It took me ages to fall asleep. I was too busy doing some remembering of my own. I wanted to recall everything I could about Gwendolyn. I couldn't wait until she got here. It felt like someone had lit a sparkler inside my chest.

I hoped she remembered me.

THe Mess Hall

Before Gwendolyn arrived, Mimi insisted we spruce up the mess hall. "We can't very well hold dance classes in the dining hall," she said.

"What's wrong with the front lawn?" Daddy asked.

Mimi gasped. "Frank! You can't mean it—"

Daddy grinned. "Of course I don't. Come on, Reenie. Let's see what kind of damage we can do."

Mimi laughed, but it sounded a bit strained. I was worried. Most of the time now she seemed happy and interested in our lives, exclaiming over Scarlett's artwork, displaying my report card on the refrigerator, asking Bo to play her a tune on his guitar. But there were still moments when the sad look on Mimi's face took my breath away.

I was happy to be doing my part, helping Daddy in the mess hall. Though sometimes I worried that I was becoming a flat-out failure as a girl. Mimi was grace and beauty and tinkling laughter, everything a woman was supposed to be. Next to her I was a mess of knees and elbows. It didn't help that every day Scarlett was growing into a mini-Mimi. It didn't seem fair that even at six years old, grace was so effortless for her. But with Daddy, I felt useful. With Daddy I could do things I knew that neither Mimi nor Scarlett could do.

"What a mess," Dad said. "I guess it lives up to its name."

We hadn't used the mess hall in ages, even for games. The dining hall had become the centre for all indoor activities. The mess hall had become an oversized storage room, a place to stash things we weren't quite ready to part with, or things Daddy had meant to fix but had never got around to. There were old picnic tables, a lawn mower that was so twisted and rusted out it looked like a demented robot, and inner tubes in need of a good patch job.

"Let's get to it."

Daddy and I spent the better part of the morning hauling things out to the lawn.

"You know this isn't the first time there will be dancing in this old place," Daddy said. "In your grandpa's time we used to hold dances here."

"Really?"

"He made me stand there all night, serving refreshments. I was excited until I realized how boring it was to watch other people dance."

Daddy pointed to the corner and I smiled, imagining him as a boy, forced to dress up and watch the grown-ups dance, itching to get out to catch fireflies or dig for worms in the dark.

"But you loved dancing with Mimi," I said.

"I did. I still do. Your mother makes every other girl look like they have two left feet."

After hours of hauling, sweeping and a good scrubbing, the mess hall was empty and full of possibility, like a blank page. Daddy and I sat on the floor at one end, considering the space. My muscles ached and sweat settled over me like a second skin, but I felt exhilarated, proud of the work we had done.

"Your mother thinks we should have a stage, so I'm going to build a platform on the far end over there. I'll build some drawers to fit underneath where we can store the chairs."

"I'll help, Daddy."

He patted my knee then hauled himself up. "You've done plenty, Reenie. You should go catch the sun before she sets. I can take it from here."

"I can help measure out the wood," I suggested, not ready to be finished. "Or hold it steady while you hammer."

"Nah, that's okay. But if you see your brother, send him this way. It won't hurt him to learn a thing or two about construction."

"But I want to help," I said, feeling as small and unimportant as a water bug.

Daddy smiled at me. "You did. I couldn't have done all this without you. Go for a swim. You've earned it. Or if you like, you could help your mother in the office."

I walked back to the lodge, his dismissal hot and heavy in my belly like a stomach ache. I paused outside the office window and peered in. Scarlett was putting on a show for Mimi, parading around the office in Mimi's high heels and an old straw hat. I couldn't hear what she was saying, but Mimi had her hands clasped in front of her face and was laughing, delighted.

I had no idea where Bo was, but decided if Daddy wanted his help so badly he could go find him himself.

I made a beeline for the beach and dug my feet into the wet sand, letting the cool water kiss my ankles while hot tears burned my eyes. I felt like a stranger in my own family.

In my opinion, Gwendolyn Cates couldn't get here fast enough.

Arrival

"They're coming! They're coming!"

Scarlett jumped to the ground from the Lookout, bending her knees deeply to cushion her fall, and then took off running across the front lawn toward the office, where I was helping Mimi sort keys at the reception desk. Mimi's hand flew to her throat.

"I wish she wouldn't do that," she muttered. "One of these days she's going to break her neck."

"No, she won't; she's a great climber!" I smiled in spite of Mimi's tone. Teaching Scarlett to climb was the only thing I taught her that seemed to stick. She didn't care a lick for caterpillars or rock hunting or canoeing, but climbing trees she loved. It was something we shared. I didn't even mind that Scarlett had adopted the Lookout as her own — letting her claim it seemed like the sisterly thing to do. Now, whenever you couldn't find her, all you had to do was look up, and there was Scarlett, straddling a branch or sitting cross-legged in the crotch of the tree.

Scarlett banged up the front steps and ran into the office, the screen door slamming behind her.

"Did you hear me?" she gasped between jagged breaths. "They're coming — I saw Daddy's car!"

"We heard you," I said.

"Is the room ready?" Mimi asked me.

I nodded. "I aired it out yesterday and made the bed this morning," I said.

"Which linens did you use?"

I blinked, not understanding the question. "The ones we always use."

Mimi looked shocked. "The flowered ones?"

"What else would I use?"

"I told you to use the guest linen."

"I did."

"That is not our guest linen; it's the linen we use for any old customer. Now go get the real guest linen out of the closet in the hall; it's light blue cotton with satin edging."

I searched my brain, but I couldn't ever remember seeing such linens, let alone using them. My good mood was beginning to sour. I had taken special care with Gwendolyn's bed, folding down the top sheet and fluffing up the pillows. It looked especially pretty in the afternoon, when the midday sunshine mellowed and poured in through the window, clear as lemon juice and just as fresh. Mimi hadn't even seen it and already she was criticizing me.

"I don't see what the fuss is about," I protested. "Daddy says we should treat all of our guests the same."

"Well, Gwendolyn is not just a guest, is she?" Mimi replied.

Before she could say anything else, a horn beeped. We both looked out the window as Daddy pulled into the lane. Mimi flapped her hands in my direction, accidentally knocking a slim vase full of forget-me-nots to the ground.

"Look what you made me do! Scarlett, go grab the mop. Reenie, you march yourself upstairs and change those linens!"

"Yes, Mimi." Scarlett hung her head like a scolded puppy and scurried off to the kitchen to fetch the mop. I raced upstairs, ripped the perfectly fine flowered sheets off the bed and remade it using the blue ones that, sure enough, I found in the closet, still encased in the box. I did the whole thing in record time, racing back downstairs just as Daddy and Gwendolyn were entering the office.

"Look who I found at the bus station," Daddy said, holding the door open with one hand and juggling a woman's suitcase and a crate full of records in the other arm. "Our very own prima ballerina!"

Gwendolyn entered; at least I thought it was Gwendolyn. The Gwendolyn I remembered from so many years ago had looked like she'd walked right out of my fairy tale book. She was silvery and ethereal, like something from another land.

But now it was hard to tell who was behind the big black sunglasses, especially with her hair wrapped up in a silk scarf in garish shades of purple, yellow and red. A sleeveless white blouse two sizes too big was tied just below her midriff, and her dancer's legs seemed to stretch on forever under her red flat-front shorts. I knew she was only four years older than I was, but suddenly the difference in our ages felt like a whole lifetime.

"Gwendolyn! You look so grown up!"

Mimi rushed forward, as if she were about to embrace Gwendolyn, but thought better of it, awkwardly taking Gwendolyn's hands in her own instead. I flushed, embarrassed for Mimi. Usually she was much more self-possessed with guests. But, as I had so recently been reminded, Gwendolyn was not *just* a guest.

Gwendolyn took off her sunglasses and hooked them on the front of her blouse, in the vee just above her bosom. It made her look hopelessly cool, like someone in a movie.

"I go by Gwen now," she said, smiling politely. "Thank you for having me."

Mimi waved it off. "Oh, no. Thank you! You're doing us a big favour, bringing some culture to the place!"

Mimi laughed, and Gwendolyn shrugged, looking uncomfortable.

"Well, I'll leave you ladies to it," Daddy said, waving and leaving us in silence. If he noticed Mimi's comment about Sandy Shores lacking culture, it didn't show. As always, he was the perfect gentleman and a gracious host. I felt a surge of pride for him and decided no city ballerina, no matter how glamorous, could be as wonderful as my dad.

We stood around, staring at each other, Gwendolyn, Scarlett, Mimi and me.

Finally, Scarlett said, "I like your scarf."

Gwendolyn reached up, as if she had forgotten she was wearing a scarf, and said, "What, this old thing?" Then she slipped it off and tossed it to Scarlett. "Here, you can have it."

Scarlett and I gaped — Scarlett, at the scarf as silky as coloured water in her hands, and I at the straw yellow curls rioting around Gwendolyn's head. Gone was the silvery hair I remembered. It had been cut, dyed, curled and sprayed solid, by the looks of it. Coupled with her red, red lips, she looked like a bona fide movie star. She was beautiful, no doubt about it, but I missed the otherworldly sheen of her hair as I remembered it.

Mimi was the first of the Starrs to recover.

"That's awfully kind of you, Gwendolyn," she said. "Now

what can we do for you, would you like some water? Lemonade? Would you like Reenie to give you a tour before dinner?"

"Please, call me Gwen," she said. "And I think I'd like to lie down for a bit. I had a late night."

"Of course! Girls?"

Gwen didn't make a move toward her suitcase. She was a girl used to having things carried for her. I didn't mind, I was a girl used to being at the service of someone else. I reached for it with one arm and found I was going to need both if I was going to manage it all the way up the stairs. I'd have to come back for the records later. Scarlett skipped ahead, waving her new scarf behind her like a flag.

"This way," I said, somewhat needlessly.

"Dinner is between five and nine in the dining hall," Mimi said. "You can come down whenever you like. We try to eat together, as a family, at six. I would love for you to join us."

"Maybe another time," Gwendolyn said. "I'm not very hungry."

She must have seen the look on my mother's face, which went from hopeful to hurt in less than three seconds, because she added quickly, "I would love to, really, it's just that I'm so tired."

Mimi brightened, the clouds that had crossed over her expression breaking up and clearing off as if they had never been there.

"Of course, forgive me. We're just so excited to have you. Now, you have a good long rest. We have all summer to get to know each other."

Something flickered across Gwen's face, but it happened so quickly I couldn't put my finger on what it was. Like Mimi, she seemed to be a master of controlling the face she displayed for the world to see. "Right," she replied.

Mimi smiled and disappeared back into the office. After she left, Gwen let out a long sigh and blew at a stray curl that had fallen over one eye.

"And so it begins," she said.

I smiled, quizzically. "What begins? Your summer?"

Gwen stared at me, searching my face; for what, I didn't know. Maybe she found it, because she smiled at me and gestured toward the stairs. "Lead on," she said.

* * *

Scarlett and I sat on the bed, watching Gwendolyn — no, Gwen — unpack. I tried not to stare, or look too interested, but I was desperate for any indication of the old Gwendolyn. That girl had been lovely, diffuse with light, like a moon princess. This girl was brash and had too many hard edges.

Her suitcase opened with a click, and the sharp, sour smell of cigarette smoke wafted into the room. It made my nose itch.

I was surprised to see the suitcase was packed solid with clothes. I had struggled carrying it to her room, thinking she must have brought books, the heavy, leather-bound kind. I had even daydreamed a little about reading together in front of the fireplace in the dining room on rainy afternoons. Maybe we would take turns reading aloud. Maybe she would introduce me to new authors.

Gwendolyn — Gwen — hummed as she unpacked, sashaying between the suitcase and the closet, holding clothes against her before smoothing them out and slipping them on hangers. Sometimes she sang a lyric or two. Most of them I didn't recognize. She didn't seem to mind that Scarlett and I were just sitting there, watching her unpack and listening to her sing. I wondered if all dancers were like that, carrying a tune and a rhythm wherever they went, ready to burst into song and dance at a moment's notice.

"I sure could use some music," Gwen said suddenly, as if she was completely unaware that she herself had been singing this whole time. "Is there a record player in here?"

"No," I said. "But there's one in the dining hall."

"What about a radio?"

"Guests usually bring their own, but there's one in the office and in the kitchen."

"And in the messy hall," Scarlett added.

"The *mess* hall," I corrected. "There's a record player there, too. That's where you'll be teaching dance. I can take you there, if you like. When you're done unpacking."

"Isn't a mess hall an army thing?" Gwen asked.

"I don't know," I admitted. "Here it's where we have games on rainy days. And now dances," I added. "I'm really excited about dance lessons. I think a lot of our guests will be."

"Great," Gwen said absently, using her teeth to break off a stray thread from the skinniest pair of pedal pushers I had ever seen.

"Do you remember me?" Scarlett asked.

Gwen smiled, but looked tired. "Yes," she sighed. "You were a cute little thing."

Scarlett looked pleased, then frowned. "I don't remember you," she said.

I rolled my eyes. "You were just a baby," I reminded her.

"But I remember Lieutenant Jesse."

"You do not, you just think you do."

"Do so!"

Gwen snorted. "Lieutenant Jesse? Who's that?" she asked. "Your dad's war buddy?"

"Lieutenant Jesse was our dog," I explained. "He died when Scarlett was three, but she claims to remember him."

"I do," Scarlett insisted. "He was all black and he used to walk beside me on the dunes so I didn't fall."

"Is that true?" Gwen asked me.

"Yes," I admitted. "But we told you about that, Scarlett. That's not the same thing as remembering it yourself."

"But I *do* remember it myself."

This was an argument that could go on forever. Gwen must have picked up on this, because she changed the subject, asking, "Why did you call him Lieutenant Jesse?"

"Mimi named him Jesse after someone in a play she saw, and Bo added the lieutenant part because he was obsessed with the war. He put lieutenant or captain in front of everything. He used to call Daddy 'Captain Dad,'" I explained.

Gwen rolled her eyes and grinned at me. I felt electrified.

"Boys," she said.

I grinned back and repeated, "Boys."

"Where is that brother of yours? The last time I saw him I showed him a thing or two about racing."

My heart leapt. So she did remember!

"He's supposed to be mowing the lawn," Scarlett said.

"But he's probably out fishing or messing around with his band," I finished.

Gwen perked up. "What kind of band?"

"Oh, they play all sorts of music," I said vaguely. The truth was I didn't know. Bo didn't consider me important enough to talk to about his band. Music was something that teenagers did, and even though I was technically a teenager, Bo didn't seem to think thirteen counted.

Out of the blue, Scarlett asked, "How come you didn't come back to visit us?"

"Scarlett, that's personal!" I scolded, smiling ruefully at Gwen, as if to say, What can you do?

I was embarrassed, but also a little jealous. Scarlett asked all the questions I wanted to know the answers to, but felt forbidden to ask. But my little sister had not yet reached the age where nosiness ceases to be cute and instead becomes a character flaw.

Gwen snorted again. "I wasn't invited."

"That's not true," I said, my face growing hot. "Of course you were invited!"

Gwen shrugged and slammed her suitcase closed, shoving it under the bed. "Well, then I guess the invitation got lost in the mail."

"You went to ballet school, you didn't have the time," I reminded her.

"It wasn't jail or anything," she said. "They gave us summers off. Although sometimes it felt like we were being punished. Look!"

Gwen sat down, swung her long legs on to the bed and displayed her feet for us to examine. Scarlett gasped. They were grey and misshapen, like troll's feet, covered in rough calluses and dried scabs. Her toes were painted candy-apple red, which made them seem that much more grotesque. I couldn't imagine them fitting into dainty ballet slippers, pink and pearly as the inside of a shell. I thought of my own feet, slim and brown and buffed smooth by the sand, and felt ill. Scarlett, however, was fascinated.

"Can I touch them?" she asked.

Gwen wiggled her toes. "Be my guest."

Tentatively, Scarlett poked at a particularly large callus running the length of Gwen's big toe.

"Ugh!" she cried, shuddering. "That's disgusting!"

"You should see the state of my nails," Gwen sighed. "That's why I always keep 'em nice and red."

"Will you paint my toenails?" Scarlett asked.

"Sure, if it's okay with your mom. The last thing I need is for someone else's mother to go all Mama Bear on me." Gwen dug around in an oversized pink plastic makeup case.

"Mimi won't mind," Scarlett assured her. "She loves makeup. She doesn't have much of it anymore, because she says it doesn't keep in the heat and the sand gets into it."

"I can do yours, too, Reenie, if you like."

"Maybe later," I said, suddenly shy.

"Suit yourself. Aha! Here we go!"

Gwen held up a small bottle of the same candy-apple red polish that tipped her own toes. She rolled it between her palms, which were smooth and white and so unlike her ruined feet.

"This keeps the air bubbles out," she explained to Scarlett.

I turned and left the room silently. All the visions I'd had of Gwendolyn and I bonding over books and late night discussions were disappearing as quickly as cotton candy on the tongue. Or, at the very least, I was being replaced by my own little sister. Just as well. If I was too old to blurt out the questions I wanted to know the answers to, I was probably too old to have someone paint my toenails.

Gwen

Gwen spent all of Monday and Tuesday in her room. I had no idea what she was doing, because not one of us disturbed her. We knew she was alive, because Scarlett and I had smelled smoke and watched from below her window as a pale arm appeared, a red-tipped cigarette dangling from lazy fingers. Everyone talked in whispers and avoided the guest room altogether, as if it held a dying invalid instead of our new dance teacher. Everyone except Scarlett, who found all sorts of reasons to walk by Gwen's room, humming softly, pausing to knock and ask if she needed anything: dinner, towels, shampoo, a swim. Each time she was met with silence.

When Gwen didn't show up for dinner for the third night in a row, Daddy let his irritation be known. Mimi told him to let her be.

"She obviously needs her sleep," Mimi said.

"I need my sleep — doesn't mean I get to lie around all day," Bo muttered.

"She's our guest," Mimi insisted.

"That may be, Dorrie, but she's also supposed to be working for us," Daddy said gently.

"Give her a few more days, Frank. She just got here."

Daddy sighed, throwing up his arms. "All right, this is your project, Dorrie. I'll leave it to you. But the girl has to eat sometime."

But Gwen *had* been eating; I knew this because I had seen her. Late Sunday night I'd heard a door open and a stair creak. I knew it couldn't be Bo or Scarlett, because we all knew which stairs to avoid when we were trying to get someplace secretly. Besides, Bo was still sneaking out through his window and across the roof. I suspected he was off meeting with shady members of his band, or else charming girls with his guitar at parties I would never be invited to.

So it had to be Gwen creeping through the halls.

I counted to ten before getting up and heading downstairs myself, veering toward the kitchen — why else would she sneak out in the middle of the night, if not for a midnight snack? I slipped from shadow to shadow, knowing the particular blackness of the lodge like the back of my hand, and watched as Gwen picked through the contents of Elsa's well-stocked fridge.

She was a disgusting eater, smothering a devilled egg with a heavy dollop of relish and sticking her fingers in the jam jar, sucking off Elsa's strawberry preserves. She took two bites out of a tomato, biting into it like an apple, before tossing it in the garbage. I had half a mind to speak out right there. *Those are Elsa's tomatoes,* I wanted to say. *She brings them from her garden. How dare you throw them away!* But then I saw her eyes. Even in the eerie glow from the refrigerator I could see how swollen they were, the edges red and raw looking. It was obvious Gwen had been crying. But why?

When she showed up at breakfast Wednesday morning, no one let on that her presence was out of the ordinary.

Everyone acted like she had been sitting down to toast and oatmeal with us for days. Even Scarlett managed to keep her surprise in check, though she had cooled to Gwen after her efforts to lure her from her room. Daddy was already in the office and Mimi poured Gwen a cup of coffee without asking, as if it were an everyday thing.

"Good morning, Gwendolyn."

"It's Gwen."

"Silly me. I keep forgetting. It's just that I've thought of you as Gwendolyn for all these years . . ."

"Feeling rested?" Bo said lightly.

Mimi sat up a little straighter, her mouth flattening into a line. Bo pretended not to see this and kept smiling at Gwen.

"Yes, thank you," Gwen said evenly. "Must be all this fresh air."

"Just wait till you get outside," Bo said dryly. "You may never wake up again."

"Actually, I did have a little trouble getting to sleep some nights," Gwen said.

Mimi looked worried. "Were you too hot?" she asked.

Gwen shook her head. "No, that's not it. Maybe it's my imagination, but I swear I heard footsteps on the roof."

Gwen stared right at Bo. Now he was the one who looked worried. I had to swallow a smile. Apparently I wasn't the only one who had heard him sneak out.

"It's probably just squirrels," Bo said, staring right back at her.

Gwen smiled at him, then at Mimi. "Probably. You must have big squirrels up here."

"Huge," Bo said, getting up to leave.

If Gwen was going to rat Bo out, it wasn't going to be today. She refused offers of toast or oatmeal and instead

nursed her coffee, smiling and nodding as Mimi fret-
ted about the squirrels. I finished my breakfast but hung
around the table, hoping to be invited to whatever Gwen
had planned for the day. When she drained the last of her
coffee, Mimi smiled and stood up.

"Now, let me get my sunglasses, and I'd be happy to give
you a quick tour, help you get reacquainted with Sandy
Shores."

My heart sank. I had been hoping to give Gwen the tour,
like I had so many years before. Entertainment may have
been Mimi's project, but tours were my specialty. As luck
would have it, Elsa popped out from the kitchen. "Excuse
me, Mrs. Starr, but we're short butter and eggs and we've got
chicken and waffles on the menu for tonight."

Mimi sighed. "Where's your father?" she asked me.

I shrugged, secretly crossing my fingers behind my back
and hoping against hope that she'd see to the groceries and
leave the tour to me.

"Fine. I'll go, Elsa. I'm sorry, Gwendolyn, but duty calls.
It's always something around here! I'll let Reenie show you
around. She's our best tour guide anyway," Mimi said, lay-
ing a hand on my head. I squirmed away from her touch.
I knew she meant it as a compliment but I couldn't help
feeling like a pet, some kind of trained guide dog. Gwen
shrugged with one shoulder.

"Sure," she said, turning her gaze on me. It was the first
time she had really looked at me this morning. I noticed
that her eyes were still blue, and they had a glint of mis-
chievousness that I remembered from a few summers ago.
"Lead on."

The Race, 1956

The first time I gave Gwen a tour was in 1956.

After years, my mother had convinced her best friend Grace to come visit, and she was bringing Gwendolyn. I couldn't wait for a new playmate, as Bo was already abandoning me and running off to play with older boys.

When she arrived at Sandy Shores, blinking in the semi-darkness of the foyer in the lodge, Gwen was exactly how I pictured a fairy princess to look: long and thin like a reed, with hair so pale it looked white. Everything about her was silvery: pale arms, light blue eyes, pearly fingernails. Her mother insisted we call her Gwendolyn, which felt as rich and exotic as Turkish delight on my tongue, a foreign candy I had never tasted but had read about in books.

I took great care to show off the best parts of Sandy Shores, all the secret parts that I knew as well as the freckles on my knee. I showed her the robin's nest nestled in the eaves of the old boathouse and pointed out every gopher's hole I knew. Despite my best efforts, including my funniest stories and as many Sandy Shores facts that I could remember, I barely got a single word from her. I told her about the progress I was making with my swimming. Like the rest of Canada, I was in love with Marilyn Bell, and I felt certain that in a few years I could beat her record and become the youngest Canadian to cross the English Channel. Surely someone who had been born only a few feet from a lake was destined to be a great swimmer.

Bo, who had been loitering around looking for frogs, offered a challenge. "Hey Weenie, I'll bet you a week's chores you can't beat me to the raft and back."

It was a mean dare and Bo knew it. The raft, a number of smooth old logs roped together and anchored to the lake bed, was at least thirty feet from the beach. I was a good swimmer and had made it to the raft many times, but Bo was three years older; there was no way I would win. I was used to this kind of unfair treatment from Bo, and I was prepared to kick up a fuss, until Gwendolyn spoke up.

"I'll race for you, Reenie."

Bo and I stared at her. I don't know what surprised me more, the sound of her voice or the fact that she was offering to swim in my place.

"You?" Bo said.

Gwendolyn shrugged her narrow shoulders. They were so thin and pointy, I imagined she had a closet full of blouses and sweaters with holes in the shoulders.

"Why not? Afraid of losing to a girl?" Gwendolyn's lip twitched, and it occurred to me that she was trying not to smile.

Bo grinned with the smug confidence of a person who knows he's about to be proven right, and said, "Sure. Weenie, you give us the go-ahead."

Bo ran off toward the edge of the beach, his heels kicking up sand in our faces. I was nervous. Gwendolyn may have been older than Bo, but she looked like she was made of ropes; the thin kind.

"Boys are such show-offs," she said to me as we made our way over the sand dunes to the beach. "Don't worry. I've been taking lessons at the pool."

Gwendolyn peeled layers of clothing off one at a time, handing them to me for safekeeping. They were warm from her skin and smelled faintly of soap. I held them close to my chest, vowing silently to keep them out of the sand and the grass until she finished the race.

"Terms are the same. If I win, Reenie still has to do all of my chores."

Gwen nodded. "But if I win, you have to do all of Reenie's chores and serve her breakfast every morning for a week."

Bo didn't even hesitate. He was that sure he would win. "Deal."

Bo spit into his hand and offered it to Gwendolyn, grinning. I gasped. The nerve! This was something I had seen Bo do all the time with his friends, but not, at least to my knowledge, with a girl; especially a city girl like Gwendolyn. But Gwendolyn spit wholeheartedly into her own palm and slapped it against Bo's, shaking vigorously. I giggled.

"Deal," she repeated. If it bothered her to have Bo's spit all over her hand, you sure couldn't tell by the way she was grinning. I wondered if, finally, Bo was about to meet his match. And better yet, in a girl!

Gwendolyn took her place in the sand next to Bo, leaning over, hands on the ground like a runner before a race. Her hair fell over her face like a curtain of moonlight. I felt a rush of pride for my beautiful, unlikely champion.

"On your marks, get set, go!"

Bo and Gwendolyn tore into the water, Bo yelling a war

cry the whole way, Gwendolyn loping like a mystical white unicorn.

I jumped and cheered as well as I could, holding an armful of clothing. It was after lunch and the sun was high in the sky, making it difficult to see. I squinted into the white glare of the afternoon as they disappeared into the water, sending up beads of water like diamonds in their wake. From my vantage point it was hard to tell who was in the lead. With her silvery hair wet and plastered to her skull, Gwendolyn looked less like a fairy princess and more like a seal, bobbing up between the waves every once in a while for air. It endeared her to me even more.

Both figures reached the raft at the same time, tagged the side, and pushed off for the final leg of the race. I screamed until my voice grew thin and my throat felt ragged. I couldn't remember the last time I had been so excited.

When Gwendolyn stood, fighting her way to the beach on foot, I couldn't believe it. She was like a mirage come to life, the Little Mermaid rising from the sea. Behind her, Bo struggled to his feet, tripped and landed with a splash. Gwendolyn ran up the beach and straight into my arms, crushing her lovely clothes between us. For such a slight person, Gwendolyn was strong. When she pulled away I was almost as wet as she was.

"Oh!" I cried. "Your clothing!"

"It'll dry," she said with a shrug. "Shall we help your brother up?"

Bo was lounging in the water, breathing heavily, grumpy as a wet cat.

"Good race," Gwendolyn said lightly. "Need a hand?"

"Sure," Bo said, pushing his wet hair out of his eyes.

"Gwendolyn, wait—" I said, but not soon enough. Bo

grabbed her outstretched hand and yanked her back into the water with him.

"Bo!" I cried, horrified, but Gwendolyn was laughing.

"What a poor sport you are," she scolded, splashing him.

"Nah, you won, fair and square," Bo admitted. "Nice job, Gwen. I guess ballet isn't the only thing you're good at."

"It's Gwendolyn," I reminded him, but Gwen didn't correct either of us. Instead, she smiled, a real smile, not one of the little polite smiles she'd been doling out since she arrived.

Gwendolyn and her mother only stayed for the weekend. Bo never did hold up his end of the deal, and without Gwendolyn there I didn't feel brave enough to insist that he did. But she was back now, for a whole summer. I would be her tour guide, her assistant and maybe — just maybe — her friend. My heart banged in my chest like it had the day of the race, full of excitement and possibility.

Dance Lessons

"And this is your studio!"

I had spent the better part of the morning showing Gwen around, saving the mess hall for last. I gave her the abbreviated version of the tour since she had been here before, but if she remembered it, she didn't let on, and neither did I.

I watched from the entrance as Gwen walked around the space. Even without curtains, which Daddy had promised to hang before the summer was out, it was an impressive space. It looked like a real performance space to me: the kind of place you could imagine seeing a concert or a play by Shakespeare. Certainly it was just as impressive as the auditorium at school. All it was missing were seats. I wanted to blurt out, "I did this," but Gwen was so calm and cool. I didn't want to act like some kid, desperate for a gold star or a pat on the head.

"This is where you'll have your classes," I explained. "The record player will sit up here, on the stage. You can jump around as much as you like, it shouldn't skip. Scarlett and I tested it before you got here. Daddy will bring in chairs later, for performances."

Just the word performance sent a shiver of delight down my spine. I imagined the place packed with people, the stage flooded in coloured lights, and I wanted to project myself five weeks into the future. I couldn't wait to see what sort of magic Gwen was going to bring to Sandy Shores.

Gwen bounced lightly on the floorboards, testing them for I don't know what. Then she spread her arms and brought them back together in a perfect circle, propelling herself across the floor like a top.

"Not bad," she said, coming to a stop.

I had to resist the urge to clap. Gwen had moved on and was inspecting a wall as if nothing had happened. Like spinning across the room was normal, something she did without thinking, like crossing her arms or snapping her gum. I wondered if all dancers burst into spontaneous movement.

"The floors will do. There's good width in here, nice light. Great windows," Gwen said. "We can open them and let a nice cross-breeze in when it gets too hot."

"The windows are my favourite part," I admitted, which was true. They were long and tall and took up half the wall space, on both sides. They reminded me of the kind of windows they put in churches, except without the bible scenes made from coloured glass. Mimi said that on already dreary days all those windows just made everything greyer, but when it's sunny the whole room glows. In early summer, when the leaves on the maples are as big as my hands, the light that filters through the trees and into the mess hall is the slightest bit green, like new peas.

"It would be nice to have a barre here," Gwen was saying, staring at a wall, holding out her hands as if she could will a bar into existence by just picturing it. At first I wondered what she would do with a bar, why the dancers would need drinks, and then I realized she was talking about the kind of bar meant for ballet. Gwen slid the toe of her left foot lightly along the ground, bringing it back against her other foot in time to a rhythm only she could feel. Even her unconscious movements were graceful. "But then again I doubt we'll be doing much ballet."

"Why not?" I asked.

"Ballet is a lot of work. People don't want to work on their vacation. And to tell you the truth, I'm kind of rusty."

"I don't believe it," I said. "Those spins were pretty good."

Gwen laughed. "No offense, but you don't know what you're looking for. I know a number of mean old biddies back home who would rap my knees for poor form."

I thought of Gwen's gnarled feet and wondered what other ugly things happened behind the scenes in the world of ballet.

"The truth is, I've been dancing less and less these days."

It was hard to imagine someone as graceful and talented as her not dancing.

"How come?"

"I've been doing a little singing."

"What kind of singing?"

"This and that. Backup, mostly."

"But you still dance, right?"

Gwen flashed me a smile that was all trouble. "Oh, I dance. Just not the kind of dancing your mother wants me to teach."

"What does that mean?"

"Can you keep a secret?"

I hesitated, only for a second. "Yes."

"I'll show you. First, we need some music. Come with me."

Gwen hurried back to the lodge to gather her records. She took the steps two at a time. It was the fastest I'd seen her move since she got here.

"You," she said, wrinkling her nose at my clothes. "Find something else to wear. Something that moves."

I searched through my drawers, pushing aside piles of ill-folded clothes. What did that mean, something that moves? All I had were blouses, dresses, jeans and a couple of stiff skirts. I didn't have time to puzzle it out. Gwen appeared a moment later, a canvas bag slung over one shoulder and an old milk crate full of albums resting on her hip.

"Oh never mind, you can use something of mine. Let's go."

We made our way back to the mess hall, Gwen racing ahead of me despite the heavy load of records in her arms. It was the kind of bright, clear day that sends people outside, no matter what chores are waiting for them at home. Not a soul was around; they were too busy soaking up the good weather at the beach. I had Gwen all to myself, and I felt sure she was going to give me my own private dance lesson. I could hardly believe my luck.

Inside, Gwen dropped the crate by the stage and started flipping through the records. "Go set up the record player, would you? I'll pick us out some tunes."

I scrambled up the stairs and dragged the record player from the wings, where it stood draped in an old blue tarp, waiting for a moment like this. Gwen was throwing open all the windows, which squeaked as they fell open, one by one. A light breeze stirred the little hairs at the back of my neck. It felt like the room was coming alive.

"Reenie, check in my bag there. See if you can find something to wear."

Gwen's bag was a jumble of coloured fabric. It looked like the mess of clothing that falls out of the dryer before you sort it. I peeled away tights, scarves, skirts and leotards. They were all warm and smelled like cigarettes and too much laundry detergent. I decided on a pink wrap skirt that looked like it was made of fine netting. Suddenly shy, I snuck off to the privacy of the wings to change. I stepped out of my cut-offs, pulled on a pair of footless tights that ended just below my knees, exposing my thistle-whipped shins to the world, and tied the skirt on. It was so long I could wrap it three times around my waist, the skirt falling in three layers, like the petals of a flower.

I emerged from the cool darkness of the wings, blinking in the sudden light. Dust motes floated lazily in the air, like snowflakes that never seemed to land. Gwen was sitting on the floor of the stage by the record player, one leg curled under and the other stretched out in front of her. Her whole body was curved over the leg. I could see the bumps of her spine like beads on a necklace, stretched across her back. I cleared my throat and she snapped up and glanced over her shoulder at me.

"Why are you still wearing that old blouse?"

I sputtered for an answer, not finding one good enough to say out loud.

"Are you wearing an undershirt?" she asked.

"Yes," I mumbled.

"Then just wear that."

Gwen switched legs and allowed herself to flop over again. I unbuttoned my blouse and lay it carefully on the stage. I was embarrassed by my undershirt, ribbed white cotton with tiny bows made of pink ribbon on the straps. It was something a little girl would wear. Paired with the pink skirt I felt like a kid playing dress-up, except that I was long past make-believe age.

"Better," Gwen said, getting to her feet. "You're going to get hot and that blouse was too restrictive in the chest."

I blushed. I didn't have much of a chest to speak of. Not compared to some girls my age, and certainly not compared to Gwen. She wasn't as buxom as some girls, but no one would mistake her for under sixteen, that's for sure.

Gwen slipped a record from its sleeve and set it gently on the turntable. A guitar started up, followed by another, and then another, as if they were motorbikes, revving their engines before a big race.

"I know this song," I said.

Gwen raised her eyebrows. "You do? I guess you're not as sweet as I thought you were."

I wasn't sure if that was a compliment. "Everyone knows Johnny Skins," I bluffed. "Isn't he kind of famous?"

Gwen laughed. "Don't tell him that. His head is big enough as it is."

"You know him?" I said.

Gwen spun away from me, her arms cutting through the dust motes like big pinwheels. "I know a lot of people," she said, a smile playing on her lips.

The guitars screamed and Johnny Skins launched into the chorus. I didn't know the lyrics, but I found my body slipping into the rhythm of the song, head nodding, toe tapping, even my heart beating in time. I couldn't help it, the song was infectious.

Gwen was watching me carefully. "You're getting into it, that's good. Now relax your shoulders and your hips. No, *relax* — like before."

I tried to relax, but it was hard to do with someone watching me. In a few long strides, Gwen was beside me, pushing down on my shoulders with her hands.

"There," she said. Then she put her hands on my hips and shook them back and forth, shaking a giggle out of me in the process.

"Sorry," I apologized. "It just feels funny."

Gwen grinned. "But it feels good, doesn't it?"

I shrugged. "I guess."

"Spread those legs!" Using her toe, Gwen kicked my legs apart. "Now I want you to imagine you're sitting back in a big saddle. You've been on a horse before, right?"

I nodded. Three, maybe four times, over at the Simpsons' farm, but I wasn't ready to ride off into the sunset or anything.

"Of course you have, you're a country girl, born and bred. Now picture yourself sitting back in that saddle, queen of the cowgirls. Shoulders back, hips relaxed, nice bend in the knee — good! You got it! Follow me."

I beamed, forgetting all about the bows on my undershirt and the state of my shins. Gwen sashayed across the room, swaying her hips one way and then the other, pausing every now and again to shake her shoulders or kick up her heels, crowing like a cowgirl. I followed, copying her bowlegged stance and cocky attitude as best I could.

"You see," Gwen called over her shoulder. "So much about dance is about feeling good in your body. This feels good, doesn't it?"

I nodded. Gwen cupped her hand around her ear.

"I can't hear you!" she called.

"It feels good!" I shouted over the music, laughing.

Gwen shimmied her way back to the record player, lifted the needle and stuffed Johnny Skins back into his sleeve, muttering, "That's enough of you, you big show-off."

The silence was sudden and deafening, as if Johnny and his motorcycle guitars had blotted out all other sound in the world.

"Don't stop; keep going," Gwen called, her voice ringing in the silence. "I want you to keep that cowgirl feeling into this next song."

The needle dropped and the swelling of violins filled the room. I paused in my strutting, bringing my legs back together, wanting to waltz or pirouette or do something grand, but Gwen called, "No, no, don't forget your inner cowgirl!"

I stumbled, caught between the saddle and the ballroom. "But the music," I protested.

"What about it?" Gwen asked.

"It's so — formal."

"So stand tall, but remember that looseness in your joints."

It was tricky, but I managed it. Gwen was sweeping across the floor, arms wide and rounded, neck impossibly long and graceful. Once again, I followed her, doing my best to do what she did, when she did it. Eventually she came to a stop, dropping into a deep curtsey. I returned the gesture.

"How do you feel?" Gwen asked.

"Long," I said. "And elegant."

Gwen laughed. "Well, that's a start."

"What's next?"

Off came the violins, on went Dion and the Belmonts. Gwen hugged the album cover to her chest and kissed the image of Dion's face noisily.

"I just love this guy," she said. "Listen to that saxophone. The saxophone might just be the sexiest instrument there is. Have you ever seen a saxophone before?"

"Yes."

"Great. I want you to imagine that *you* are the saxophone."

Gwen ran her hands down my sides, saying, "Imagine there are keys on both sides of your torso. Your neck is the neck, your head is the mouthpiece and you've got this great big bell coming right out of your pelvis. That's where all the sound comes from. Got it?"

She started the song over again. I sat back in my imaginary cowgirl saddle and tapped my heels until I felt like I had swallowed the beat.

"Remember you're not playing the saxophone — I want you to *become* the saxophone."

Gwen was in her own little world, eyes closed, moving across the floor like she was made of waves, all rolling shoulders and hips. I closed my own eyes and imagined that I was the source of that cranky, husky sound, shuddering up and down the melody. When the music ended, I opened my eyes, surprised at how out of breath I felt.

Gwen clapped. "There you go, Reenie, lesson number one; if it feels good, do it."

king of the campfire

Now that Gwen had emerged from her self-imposed seclusion, Mimi wanted to talk about her plans for the summer.

"What sort of classes do you think you'll teach?" she asked.

Gwen shrugged. "Whatever you want me to teach," she said.

Mimi tried again. "That's very accommodating of you, but you are the one teaching, after all. I want you to be comfortable here, teaching what you would like to teach."

Gwen's eyes found mine over her glass of milk, just for a split second. I felt my cheeks heat up with our secret. "Anything?" she said lightly.

I had to look away, stuffing my mouth full of cheesy broccoli.

"Nothing too hard. I doubt you'll have many advanced dancers," Mimi admitted, "but I think you'll find our guests very interested in all kinds of dance. Maybe some waltzes, or something fun, like the jive?"

Bo smirked. "Maybe you can teach everyone the bunny hop," he suggested.

Mimi flushed. "That's not what I meant, I want you to teach real dances. Bo, don't be such a kidder. Gwen is a professional—"

"Actually, I'm not exactly—" Gwen started, but Mimi cut her off sharply, her voice hard and full of disdain.

"You're the closest this place has ever seen and probably ever will see."

"What's wrong with the bunny hop?" Daddy joked, trying to smooth things over. "That sounds like the kind of dance I can handle."

"The bunny hop is for babies, Daddy," Scarlett said solemnly. "Even I know that."

We all went back to our plates, the Starrs plus one, filling the silence with the sounds of eating. Gwen spoke first.

"I was thinking I could teach kids' classes in the mornings, a few adult classes in the afternoons and then hold a dance on Friday nights."

"Wonderful!" Mimi said. "That's exactly what I had in mind, too."

"We have campfire on Friday nights," Bo pointed out.

"We have campfire every night," Mimi said. "One night less isn't going to make a difference."

"But it's the last night for some people. They are going to expect a campfire."

That's when Daddy chimed in. "Why can't we have both? The dance can go from eight to nine, campfire at nine fifteen."

Mimi beamed, reaching for Daddy's hand. "Perfect. That's why you're the boss around here."

After dinner, Gwen followed Bo into the kitchen, carrying

her plates. I was already at the sink, hastily scrubbing my own dishes so I could go out and catch a swim before the sun went down.

"Look, I wasn't trying to take over your show or anything," she started, but Bo dumped his dishes in the soapy water, sending foamy suds everywhere, including the front of my blouse and Gwen's arms.

"Hey!" I cried, but Bo didn't even flinch. As always, I was invisible to him.

"Don't worry about it," he said, brushing past her. "It's fine."

I wrung the edge of my blouse in the sink, glowering.

"Moody, isn't he?" Gwen said.

I smiled, in spite of my wet shirt and soured mood. "Musicians," I said.

Gwen rolled her eyes. "Tell me about it."

*   *   *

The Sandy Shores family campfire was a tradition that had started when Daddy was small. Even now the whole family was expected to take part, which we all did happily. Campfire was not something anyone wanted to skip. It was the thing I missed most in the winter, when the lake was choked with ice and everything I loved was sleeping under a few feet of damp, heavy snow. If you stare long enough into the fire, all the noise in your head that builds up during the day disappears and the only thing that is left is peace. After campfire, I would try to make it the whole way home without saying a single word, not wanting to break the spell. It's almost like sleepwalking.

Because the Sandy Shores campfire was a family affair, there were no ghost stories, but there was lots of singing — Daddy said it was the heart and soul of a good campfire.

With his guitar, he walked in the rows between the logs and the chairs and sang. His wasn't the prettiest voice, but he sang loudly and with feeling. It was almost impossible not to join in. When you did, he nodded at you, smiling with his eyes, and you felt special to be part of the chorus.

My job was to go from person to person, offering roasting sticks that I had collected. The whole summer, everywhere I went I was on the lookout for another great roasting stick — long, slim branches hidden in the brambles or blown into the road by the wind. I only took sticks that had fallen to the ground by nature's accord; it was bad luck to break a perfectly healthy branch off a tree. I found my best ones scattered in the woods after a bad storm.

As I passed out the sticks, Scarlett followed along behind me, clutching a bag of marshmallows nearly as big as she was. Her hair was curled up around her head in a wild mess of curls that, as someone pointed out, made her look just as sweet as Shirley Temple. Bo taught her to sing a couple of Shirley Temple songs as she passed out the marshmallows. Even those women who claimed to be watching their figures and swore they wouldn't eat a single roasted marshmallow were charmed into taking seconds and sometimes thirds.

Bo started running the campfire last year, and it was an arrangement that made everyone happy. Daddy was satisfied that Bo was taking an interest in the business of Sandy Shores, and Bo found a way to help out that he actually enjoyed. The guests were thrilled. Night after night, I heard them whisper to each other about how special he was, what a talent; how he lived up to his last name, Starr. They even gave him a nickname: King of the Campfire.

As Bo got older and became more and more of a stranger at Sandy Shores, he still showed up every night for campfire.

Whatever turbulence was stirring Bo up on the inside was calmed by the fire, and he was the same old Bo again, smiling and laughing and good with a song. That was one more thing I loved about the Sandy Shores family campfire: there was no use pretending to be something else — you couldn't look into the flames and be anything but yourself.

No wonder Bo was angry about the dances cutting into the campfire.

HOW TO BE a Teenager

I became Gwen's unofficial assistant, helping her pick the best times for her classes, designing posters to hang up in the office and the lodge. At first Mimi tried to join in, chatting about Gwen's ballet classes and recalling her days as a chorus girl in Toronto. Gwen was polite about it, but I was annoyed. We couldn't become the kind of friends I wanted us to be with Mimi hanging around. We were the kids, she was the adult. Why didn't she see that? Why couldn't she just act like a mother for once?

I came up with more and more tasks that took us away from the lodge, where Mimi was stuck most days in the office. I decided Gwen needed to be properly introduced to our guests. We went from cottage to cottage and even walked up to guests lounging in big sunglasses on bright towels by the water. Gwen stood off to one side, looking beautiful and mysterious, while I gave everyone the sales pitch.

"Gwen has come all the way from a dance school in

Toronto to bring a touch of class to Sandy Shores," I said. Gwen rolled her eyes the first time I said it.

"A touch of class?" she said with a laugh. "We'll see about that."

But everyone seemed to buy it. I could tell by the way their eyes slid over her that they were just as enchanted as I had been the first time I met her. Even in her heavy makeup and crunchy curls, there was still a touch of the fairy princess that had taken my breath away so many years ago.

I sat in on all of her classes. At first I pretended to be there on official Sandy Shores business, sweeping the floors, cleaning the windows, de-cobwebbing the wings, pouring everyone glasses of water from a cool pitcher when they were thirsty. But eventually I gave up the busywork and sat down to watch. Sometimes I changed records or let Gwen move my arms around like a puppet master if she needed a person to demonstrate with.

Afterwards, I stayed behind and helped Gwen clean up. She tried to shoo me away once, but I insisted on staying. Sometimes she gave me private lessons. And not just dance lessons; Gwen was teaching me how to be a teenager. It seemed to me that some people woke one day knowing how to act and what was cool, like Bo and now Gwen. But before Gwen took me under her wing, I felt like I had spent my first year as a real teenager in a foreign country where everyone knew the language but me. Now I had a personal tutor. And not just any tutor: the star pupil.

We went through her music collection, record by record. There was a story behind every band, every song, and Gwen seemed to know them all. I read the liner notes, lying on my stomach on the empty stage, while Gwen paced back and forth, sometimes breaking into a dance step. She may have claimed that she wanted to be a singer, but she had dancing in her bones.

"Now this is Frankie Valli and the Four Seasons. He's a bit of a pipsqueak if you ask me, but have you ever heard anyone sing like that?" Gwen held out her arm. "Look! I've got goosebumps!

"This is The Shirelles. They really know what they're talking about. Listen to the lyrics. So many songs claim to be about love, but they're just full of the kind of empty promises boys *think* you want to hear. They don't sing about anything that matters. But The Shirelles know what matters. They're the real deal."

Gwen had lots to say about love and boys in general.

"Do you have a boyfriend?" I asked.

Gwen twisted a gold band around her finger, but didn't say anything.

"Did he give that to you? Is it a promise ring?"

Gwen sighed. "It's a long story, Reenie."

"I don't mind."

"Don't you have somewhere to be? Friends your own age you can go swimming or get into trouble with?"

I shrugged, pretending to be engrossed in the lyrics printed on the inside of the album cover.

"What do you do for fun out here?"

"This is fun," I said.

Gwen snorted and flung herself dramatically across the stage. "If this is fun, then I must have died and woke up in hell."

I didn't say anything, but I didn't have to. I forgot I was with a body language expert. Gwen said that dance was like a language and your body told the story. She took one look at my stiff body and immediately apologized. "Oh, hey look, I didn't mean anything by it. You know I like hanging out with you, it's just, nothing happens here. Everyone spends all day sunning themselves on the beach and then goes to bed at nine. I'm a city mouse, Reenie, holed up in the countriest of places. It makes me dull as a doornail. Surely there are other people you'd rather spend your free time with than sad old me?"

"I haven't had much luck in the friend department," I admitted.

"I don't believe it," Gwen said. "There isn't one person around here you'd want to be friends with?"

I thought about the girls I knew from school. I was always invited to birthday parties, and I never lacked for a partner when it came to school projects, but there wasn't a particular girl that I could call my best friend. Most of them were nice enough, except for Donna Struthers, but nobody really liked her anyway. Anyway, Sandy Shores was almost an hour from Orillia, not really close enough to pop by someone's house on a whim, and I was so busy during the summer and fall season that I didn't have time to think about anything else. I had my family and Sandy Shores, and they had always seemed to be enough before.

But now I had Gwen, and I'd started to wonder what I'd been missing without a best girl friend.

"Not really," I said. "Laura Jones is nice. And Maryanne Black, I guess."

"You should call them."

"Just out of the blue?"

Gwen shrugged. "Why not? I bet they'd love to come spend the day with you here. How many other girls can offer a beach, a fire pit and a full-service dining hall?"

"I guess. But they hang out with Donna Struthers. I don't like her at all."

"Why not?"

"She's mean. She makes fun of Sandy Shores in front of everyone."

"What does she say?"

I hugged my knees to my chest, remembering some of the awful things Donna had said. "She's always calling it a campground, like it's something dirty or ordinary, and when we were in grade four she told people that the sewage backed up and our beach was contaminated. People called it Smelly Shores for ages."

"She's probably just jealous."

"I doubt it. Her family has the nicest house in Orillia. They even have a trampoline in the backyard." I scuffed my toe on the floor and continued. "Plus she's always trying to make me look stupid. Once she invited me to her house at six-thirty but told everyone else to come at six. When I got there, they had already eaten dinner and she made it seem like I was late, like she hadn't lied to me from the beginning." Retelling that story made my cheeks burn and my chest hurt. I bet no one ever played tricks like that on Gwen.

"Well that Donna sounds like a real bitch."

I must have looked as shocked as I felt, because Gwen took one look at me, leaned over and whispered, "I'm not a saint, you know. You're always looking at me like I'm a princess. It gives me the heebie-jeebies. Relax, would you? I'm just a regular girl, like you." Gwen downed the rest of her Coca Cola before letting out a large belch. I giggled.

"You're the strangest ballerina I ever met," I said.

Gwen swatted me on the shoulder. "Even ballerinas burp," she said.

"Don't let Mimi catch you," I said. "Burping OR swearing."

Gwen gasped and fluttered her eyelashes. "I wouldn't dream of it. She'd probably keel over and die." We both laughed, then Gwen continued, "You know what your problem is, Reenie Starr? It's not lack of rhythm or clothing or even that bitch Donna Struthers."

I giggled nervously. I wasn't used to hearing language like that said aloud, even if it was true.

Gwen continued. "Your problem is that you don't believe that you're capable of something spectacular."

friday Night wars

It was no secret that Bo was not happy about Gwen's Friday night dance cutting into his campfire time. In fact, Bo didn't seem to like anything about Gwen's presence at Sandy Shores. He made a point to comment on her absence at meals, and when she showed up he refused to speak to her or anyone else, grunting instead of replying and eating as fast as he could in order to leave the table before anyone else had finished. Gwen didn't seem to care, she barely noticed Bo, but Mimi certainly did.

"Bo, I'd like you to clear the table tonight."

"I thought we were all responsible for clearing our own dishes," Bo said.

"I've changed my mind," Mimi said icily. "I want you to do it for the rest of the week."

"Am I being punished for something?"

"Yes. For rudeness. Gwen is our guest and you've barely gotten to know one another. You're almost the same age, you

90

both like music, surely you can find something to talk about."

"Fine. So, Gwen. How do you feel about Elvis?"

Mimi's eyes flashed. "Bogart, I did not raise you to be insincere."

Bo flinched at the sound of his full name, but didn't apologize. Instead he stood up, grabbed everyone's plates and thundered into the kitchen. Mimi sighed, pinching the bridge of her nose.

"Please forgive him, Gwen. I know there isn't any excuse, but I—"

Gwen shrugged, cutting her off. "Don't sweat it, Mrs. Starr. Boys will be boys. I've known worse, believe me."

Gwen didn't have any siblings and I wondered what kind of company she was keeping that she could brush off Bo's bad behaviour so easily. One scathing look or offhand comment from Bo and I felt as low as an earwig. But she barely seemed to notice him. It made me respect her even more.

I didn't realize just how bull-headed Bo was until he missed the first Friday night dance. He may have had a problem with Gwen, but it was important to Mimi that all of the Starrs come out to support her project. Daddy washed up and made an appearance, twirling her around the mess hall a few times, and Scarlett had a ball running around giggling with some of the other kids. I was supervising the refreshments, knowing full well that no one was about to ask me to dance. It felt better to be useful, handing out lemonade and dessert bars.

The first night went off without a hitch, but I could tell Gwen was a little disappointed. "It was the music," she said. "Too old-fashioned. We need to liven it up a little. Next week will be different."

True to her word, the following Friday, Gwen played all

her favourite records, filling the mess hall with fast, loud music and dancing — "The Twist," "The Locomotion," "The Wah-Watusi." At first I was concerned that people wouldn't approve, some of our guests were much older and probably spent many evenings listening to classic music programs on the radio. But everyone seemed to be having a good time.

The mess hall was packed with people, hot but smiling, and thoroughly enjoying themselves. Men rolled up their shirt sleeves and a few women even kicked off their shoes. Everyone was having such a good time that no one stopped by the refreshment table. I helped myself to three sticky lemon bars before they melted into a gooey mess.

I didn't realized how much time had passed until Bo barrelled through the doorway. It was then that I saw that it was dark out, well past sunset, which meant that campfire should be going strong. I could tell from behind the refreshment table that Bo was going to blow his top. He made a beeline for Gwen, who was seated on the edge of the stage, legs swinging, and he started yelling. I couldn't hear him over the music, so I left my post and edged closer to them.

"Do you have any idea what time it is?" he shouted.

Gwen looked innocent. "How could I? As you can see, there is no clock in the mess hall."

"It's quarter to ten," he said.

"So?"

"So campfire was supposed to start half an hour ago."

I looked around. The mess hall was still full. People had either forgotten about campfire or decided it wasn't as much fun as the dance. Bo narrowed his eyes and shook his finger in Gwen's face.

"I think you know exactly how late it is. I think you did this on purpose."

"Of course I did it on purpose," Gwen said lightly, pausing to flip the record. "It *is* my job, you know. Your mother hired me to come here and hold dances. If you have a problem, you can take it up with her, although something tells me she'll be on my side. Look at her — she's practically the life of the party!"

It was true. Mimi was having a wonderful time, moving between the groups of people, her cheeks flushed and sweaty, laughing brightly. Bo passed a hand over his face as if he could wipe the scene from his eyes.

"Look, you've been here for less than a month. You don't know how anything works. Campfire is what we do. It's tradition. I know you don't understand that, but—"

Gwen's eyes flashed. In a moment she went from lightly teasing to full on cussing him out.

"I understand more than you think. I understand that you can't stand that these people would rather be here dancing in this stuffy old hall than grovelling at your feet at the nightly Bo Show."

My jaw dropped. No one spoke to Bo like that.

Gwen continued, "Say all you like about tradition and responsibility. I don't believe you. As far as I can tell, you come and go as you please, without a second thought to anyone but yourself. You don't care about Sandy Shores tradition, all you care about is that there will be less people mooning over you and your guitar." Gwen shook her head, disgusted. "At least I *know* I'm a princess. You're the worst kind of spoiled brat, the kind who doesn't know how lucky he is and spits on the people who worship him."

At that moment, Mimi arrived, completely oblivious to the situation. Bo was glaring at Gwen so intensely, I was sure that anyone who stepped between them would fall down dead, electrocuted by the hate zinging between them.

"Gwen, do you think you could put on one of the waltzes you've been working on? Or perhaps the cha-cha? Some of the ladies want to show their husbands what they've learned."

Gwen smiled brightly. "Sure thing, Mrs. Starr," she said.

Mimi smiled gratefully and gave her elbow a squeeze before disappearing back into the crowd. Bo shook his head, glaring.

"You are unbelievable," he said.

Gwen put two fingers into her mouth and whistled. A hush fell over the mess hall and people craned their necks to see what the big deal was, why the music had stopped. Gwen smiled at everyone and motioned for them to be quiet.

"Hi, everybody! Thank you so much for joining us tonight. I just want to let you know this is the last song of the evening." The sound of people protesting and calling for more was so loud that Gwen had to stop for a moment before continuing. "Now, now, it doesn't mean the night is over! One more song, then we'll all head over to the fire pit to be entertained by the one, the only, Mr. Bo Starr."

Gwen gestured to Bo, who smiled sheepishly at the enthusiastic applause he received from the crowd.

"This is the last song; make it a good one!" She changed the record and hopped lightly off the stage, eye-to-eye with Bo. "Happy now?" she said.

He was speechless.

"Look, I'm not trying to ruin anything," Gwen said. "I'm just trying to get through the summer, same as you are."

Bo shook his head and walked away without so much as a thank you. Gwen was right about a lot of things, but she was wrong about summer. Bo might be a champion at avoiding chores and spending all day with his guitar, but he wasn't trying to get through anything. Bo is a Starr; we don't get through the summer, we live for it.

* * *

As much as she enjoyed ruffling Bo's feathers, Gwen was always on her best behaviour at campfire. She'd been making sporadic appearances, but I was glad to see her that night. Her sitting there was like a peace offering.

Sometimes I sat beside her, but that night I sat across from her, at my usual spot next to Bo. It was easier to watch her from there. I was fascinated by her campfire transformation. Gwen seemed to melt into the crowd in a way I wouldn't have thought possible. All day long she stood out, like a movie star dropped into the middle of the woods, but at night she lost her shine and became another anonymous reveller at the Bo Show. And, thanks to her, that's what I began to call it: the Bo Show. I wouldn't have said it out loud, but it felt good just thinking it.

Generally, Gwen stayed for the whole thing, but a few times she got up and left. I would watch as she disappeared into the darkness, and then as her light appeared in the upstairs window. I'd wonder what was wrong, what had made her leave. Gwen's sadness fascinated me. I wanted to know what took away her appetite and made such a lively, fun person curl up inside herself. Maybe I could help her. Part of me wanted to get up and follow her, but I knew no matter how much I knocked, she would probably ignore me. Besides, I had responsibilities at campfire.

After about twenty minutes of the usual singalong songs, Bo cleared his throat.

"All right, folks, if you'd be so kind as to indulge me, I

have a new one I'd like to try out on you tonight."

The crowd murmured assent and Bo started strumming lightly, leaning over his guitar like it was something precious. Lately Bo had been introducing some of his own songs. They were pretty, mostly about love, with a catchy tune that showed off Bo's voice nicely. It was hard to believe that my brother had so many things to say on the subject. I wondered if he was singing about one girl in particular. Just thinking about it made me feel weird, as if I had been caught reading his diary, not that Bo kept one. Besides, why should I feel guilty when he was putting his feelings out there for the world to hear? I couldn't believe that it was based on someone, but how could he write such beautiful songs about something he hadn't experienced?

Watching Gwen, I wondered if she had experienced some of the ups and downs that Bo was singing about. As the light and shadow of the flames passed over her face she was one moment sad and the next at peace. What was running through her mind? Was it the song that made her sad, or something else?

People fell quiet when Bo was singing his own songs, partly out of respect but mostly because they had never heard them before. But then, out of nowhere, someone joined in, adding a layer of harmony, like the sweet white glaze on a lemon cake.

I looked up, searching for the mystery singer. It was Gwen. Bo was looking at her as well, but he didn't frown. He didn't even look all that surprised. He just nodded slightly and kept going. When they finished he didn't even acknowledge her, or mention her by name. I suppose he didn't need to. All our guests knew who Gwen was, if only by sight. No one could rival her long legs or butter-yellow curls.

As people drifted back to their beds, Gwen hung around while we cleaned up. I raked the fire pit, burying the last glowing embers, and collected the roasting sticks while Bo tuned his guitar. I wondered how long she would stand there, hands tucked under her armpits, balancing on one leg, like a beautiful stork, watching us.

"I like that song," she said eventually. "That last one. It's pretty."

Bo didn't look up from his guitar. "Thanks," he said.

Gwen waited for him to say something else, but when he didn't she turned to walk away. She didn't get six feet when he added, "I liked the harmony you added."

Gwen smiled. "Thanks," she said.

From that night forward, an uneasy peace was achieved between them. Bo said hello to her in the mornings and Gwen stopped mentioning Bo's midnight excursions. They weren't exactly friendly, but they were polite. Campfire was the only time they really seemed to get along. They sounded nice, like they had being singing together their whole lives.

Letters and Silverware

With Gwen around, I had been neglecting some of my regular Sandy Shores duties, but I still collected the mail. Every day after lunch I made the trek to the end of the lane, where Daddy had nailed a silver mailbox to a post. It was dented and scratched and looked like it had been through more than a few hurricanes, but the latch was strong and the little red flag still stood at attention after the mailman had made his delivery. After years of mail collecting, I could tell what was a regular old bill and what was a letter for a guest by the weight of the envelope alone. At some resorts, guests could pick up their mail at the office, but we were small enough to hand deliver it. That's how I knew that Gwen was receiving mail — and lots of it.

The first letter arrived days after she did. I resisted the urge to study the return address. Respecting our guests' privacy is very important at Sandy Shores. But Gwen was such a mystery to me that I thought a peek couldn't hurt. If anything, it might give me a clue to her strange behaviour.

As the weeks passed, Gwen received a number of creamy white envelopes about the size of a birthday invitation, with her mother's name — Mrs. Grace Cates — stamped in gold ink on the back. But who were the other letters from? The handwriting was spiky and looked rushed, addressed with a pen that seemed to have been running out of ink. The first initial was a wild and loopy cursive letter G, or possibly a J, but the last name was barely more than a scrawl. It was a short name, but I could never quite make it out. The rest of the letters might as well have been Egyptian hieroglyphics; they were nearly impossible to decipher.

Even the stamp was on an angle. I noted letters from Detroit, Michigan, even New York, all addressed in the same messy handwriting. Gwen was always telling me stories about the parties and concerts she went to, but she never mentioned any close friends. Even when she did mention a name, it never came up more than once. I would know. I was constantly taking mental notes about Gwen's life as a dancer in the big city. If not her mother or a friend, the mystery letters had to be a boyfriend of some sort. But why had she never mentioned him?

If Gwen was in her room, she snatched the mail from me, tossing the envelopes from her mother on the dressing table — one more for her growing collection of unopened letters from home. But the ones with the illegible handwriting she ripped into right away. I knew enough to leave immediately. The first time I'd lingered, and she'd glared at me and asked, "What's a girl got to do to get some privacy around here?"

On the afternoons that Gwen received mail from the writer with the scraggly writing, her classes suffered. She became more like her hated ballet teachers: sticking with the same record, making her students repeat the simplest exercises until she was satisfied, and never smiling or joking as she came around to adjust their positioning. She wouldn't take requests for music or tell any funny stories about life in ballet school, and she certainly didn't allow a free dance song at the end of the lesson.

Gwen's behaviour made everyone nervous and jittery, which made it harder for them to ground themselves and master the movements. This led to wobbling and falling out of position, which only shortened her temper even more. Their eyes darted toward me as if I could do something. I smiled helplessly and shrugged my shoulders, as if to say, "We're all in the same boat." But even though that was true, it's not how the guests saw it. I was a Starr, my family ran this place. Surely I could do or say something.

Daddy always said the curse of the hospitality business is that people expect you to be able to fix everything. "When it rains, they look at you like it's your fault. We can't control the weather, Reenie, but we can offer people an umbrella."

At the end of one of these lessons, after Gwen had stormed off, I poured glasses of water for the guests and talked brightly about what an opportunity it was to be taught by a professional ballerina. "Isn't it something that she treats us like real ballet students — challenging us instead of treating us like amateurs?"

"But we are amateurs," Mrs. Higgins said, mopping her brow with the back of her hand. She was so pink she looked parboiled. I couldn't tell if it was the heat or embarrassment; Gwen had said a number of unflattering things about the state of her pliés.

Elinor Higgins was a Sandy Shores regular. But, despite her loyalty, she was the kind of person who was used to

SUMMER DAYS, STARRY NIGHTS

being catered to. A few more lessons like this and word would definitely get back to Mimi. Or worse, Daddy. Gwen was the closest thing I had to a friend here. At the very least she kept things interesting. I wasn't ready to let stuffy old Elinor Higgins get her in trouble.

"But isn't it something to be *treated* like professionals?" I went on, as if treating people coldly and with disdain was professional and being kind and funny was not. I'm not sure anyone bought it.

That night, as I'd feared, Mrs. Higgins cornered Mimi in the dining hall to complain about "that Nazi ballerina." I was glad Gwen had decided to skip dinner and was out of earshot. Mimi voiced concern and promised to look into it, adding, "Maybe that's how they do things in the big city, but out here we're a lot more congenial."

I noted she didn't take any blame, nor did she say Gwen was in the wrong. Clearly I wasn't the only one who listened when Daddy lectured about customer service in the hospitality industry.

* * *

The next morning, Mimi stopped me on my way to the mess hall.

"Reenie, I was hoping you could help me this morning."

"With what?"

"The silverware needs polishing."

My heart sank. On my list of most hated chores, polishing the silverware was number two, right after cleaning the bathroom. It made me feel like Cinderella, except there was no fairy godmother to swoop in and save the day. We never even used the silverware. It was a wedding gift, meant for special occasions that never happened.

"Fine," I sighed.

Mimi and I sat across from each other in the office, forks, spoons and knives spread out between us. Outside I could see the morning sunlight glinting off the lake. I sighed. The silver of the heavy old utensils could never compare to the silver of the lake. My hands were grimy and the smell of the silver polish burned my nose.

"You've been spending a lot of time with Gwendolyn," Mimi said.

"She goes by Gwen now."

"Of course, I keep forgetting that. I hope you're not bothering her."

My face felt hot. "Why would I be bothering her?"

Mimi frowned. "She's a lot older than you are, Reenie. It's very nice of her to befriend you like she has, but I'm not sure it's entirely appropriate."

"But she wants to hang out with me. We're friends."

"I'm sorry. I was just curious. What do you talk about?"

"All sorts of things."

"Does she ever mention getting back into ballet?"

"Who says she's not doing ballet right now?"

"She dropped out of her ballet classes."

I tried to remember if Gwen had told me this, but she talked in hints and suggestions. I knew she had been pursuing her musical interests, but it had never occurred to me that she had quit ballet altogether.

"Oh, really?" I said.

Mimi sighed. "Poor Grace. All those lessons, all that money down the drain. She's worried about Gwendolyn."

"It's *Gwen*."

Mimi looked up from the knife she was polishing. "I'm not sure I like that tone, Maureen."

I bristled, but apologized. It was easier that way.

"This is exactly my point. I don't want you picking up bad behaviour from her."

"I said I was sorry," I pleaded.

To my surprise, Mimi smiled. "No, I'm sorry. I've kept you in on our most beautiful morning yet and then badgered you with questions. Go. I'll finish up here."

"Really?" I asked, backing slowly toward the door, in case she changed her mind.

"Really. But Reenie, just because Gwen is here, doesn't mean you can forget about your Sandy Shores duties."

"I won't."

"I'd like you to spend one afternoon a week in the office."

That meant one less afternoon with Gwen, in the studio, listening to music and learning about dance. I felt like I was being punished, but I didn't know what I had done wrong. Still, it could be worse. I bit the inside of my cheek and nodded, dutifully. It wouldn't do to be petulant now.

"Okay. When do I start?"

"This afternoon."

"Fine," I sighed. "Can I go now? If I hurry, I won't miss the first class."

Mimi smiled. "You're really taking to dance," she said. "I'm glad. I used to love it — I studied it a little when I was living in Toronto."

A wistful expression settled over her face, and I left as quickly as I could. One second longer and Mimi would launch into one of her tales about being a struggling actress in the city. Her stories were losing their sheen; they didn't feel as magical to me anymore. I'd rather hear Gwen talk about ballet school, or the clubs she had snuck into to see bands play. Mimi's stories were in the distant past. Like her photographs, they were old and yellowing, moments stuck in time. But Gwen's stories were vibrant and full of life. I could picture the smoky clubs and ornate dance halls where she'd tried her first cigarette or flirted with much older men. Those stories were going on right now; Gwen's life was more real to me than Mimi's had ever been.

A New Student

A week later I was sitting cross-legged on the stage, trying to bring my nose to my toes in a daily struggle to improve my flexibility, when Gwen said, "Well, what do you know. Look, ladies! We have a special guest."

I glanced up, thankful for the distraction, and saw Mimi hovering near the entrance to the mess hall. I stifled a gasp. It was her, but she looked totally different. She was dressed for class, in a black leotard with a filmy skirt knotted at her waist. Even her hair was smoothed back and pinned securely in a bun. I had never seen those clothes before; she must have kept them from her years in Toronto as a chorus girl. She looked fifteen years younger. A knot formed in my heart, hard as stone. If she had all these dance clothes, why hadn't she offered me something to wear when I started taking Gwen's classes? I could be dressed like a real dancer, but instead I was wearing old undershirts and Gwen's cast-offs, while Mimi stood there looking like she had just walked off the set of a ballet movie.

Mimi closed the door behind her, smiled at the guests and waved to Gwen.

"Don't mind me," she said. "I've heard such lovely things, I thought I would come check out a class. That is, if it's all right with you, Miss Cates?"

I immediately thought of Elinor Higgins and what a spiteful old cow she was. I wondered if this had been all her idea.

Gwen looked at her students: seven women, a sour-looking girl who was probably a year or so older than I was, and an eleven-year-old keener who took ballet during the year and insisted on taking both the children's and adult classes to "maintain her form."

"Are we okay with the boss lady joining us today?" she asked with a smile. When no one spoke up, Gwen gestured to Mimi. "Sure thing, Mrs. Starr. We're just about to start our pliés."

"Wonderful."

Mimi took her place in the back row, standing a little apart from the others, looking both elegant and nervous. If she saw me, she certainly didn't let on. I flopped back over my thighs, stretching my back as far as I could stand the pinch.

Gwen led us in a series of pliés, followed by tendus and développés. Normally I was very good at keeping my balance, but I kept spying Mimi out of the corner of my eye and toppling to one side.

"Ground yourself, Reenie," Gwen called from the floor. "Imagine you're a tree, reaching tall but grounded all the way through the spine."

My cheeks flamed as Mimi and I made eye contact. She definitely knew I was there now.

Gwen walked through the dancers, adjusting their postures. She paused in front of Mimi.

"Very nice, Mrs. Starr. I heard you used to be a dancer."

"Please, call me Mimi. I was more of an actress, really. But I was in the chorus of a musical comedy, once. I had a wonderful time. All those girls crammed into a single dressing room . . . we were thick as thieves. After the show we would go to Fortelli's for dinner. Do you know that place? Real, home-cooked Italian food. You've never seen bigger plates of pasta."

"Can't say that I know a Fortelli's, Mrs. Starr, but your form is great. Look at this, ladies, almost twenty years and three kids later and Mrs. Starr is still living up to her name."

The women smiled and clapped politely. Mimi was caught between wanting to disappear and wanting to bask in all that attention. Gwen's compliments were genuine, even if they did highlight Mimi's age and the fact that she had left that life behind. My jaw ached from clenching it. This was my space, and Mimi was taking it away from me. Couldn't Gwen see she was here to check up on us?

As angry as I was, I couldn't stop staring. The only dancing I'd seen Mimi do was with Daddy, who would sweep her across the floor in a rhythm-less waltz. This was real dancing, the kind Gwen had been trying to teach me for weeks, and Mimi seemed to step back into it as if it were an old slipper.

I wasn't the only one who was mesmerized. Gwen found all sorts of reasons to adjust her form or offer her tips, and not just because she was her boss, but because she was truly impressed. She ignored everyone else and spent every spare moment at Mimi's side. They looked like two peas in a pod, with their long arms perfectly rounded over their blond heads, tilted just so. It was that particular angle, haughty but somehow beautiful, that I could never master. Yet there was my mother, easing back into it as if it were something she was born to, while I had to submit to Gwen twisting my head this way and that, frowning at me like I was a painting that didn't make any sense.

When the class ended, I poured everyone a glass of water, as always, and forced myself to make cheery comments on their progress. It occurred to me that this was the kind of thing my mother should be doing, since this whole dance class was supposed to be her project. She should be the assistant, and I should be the student. Instead, she was monopolizing Gwen, chatting about ballet as if she still had something relevant to say after all these years.

"Thank you, Gwen. That was wonderful. I feel years younger. You really are a good teacher. I'm so happy this is working out."

"Come back anytime, Mrs. Starr. You've still got it!"

"You probably say that to all your students," Mimi said, but she smiled broadly.

I kept my head down and pretended to be busy flexing my feet until I heard the door shut behind her.

"You never told me your mom could dance," Gwen said.

"I guess dancing is just one more of her many talents I didn't inherit," I said bitterly.

"Don't be like that. You're getting much better."

"She can't stand that I'd rather hang out here with you and now she's checking up on me."

"I think it's more likely that she's checking up on me," Gwen said.

I had half a mind to let Gwen know that was exactly what Mimi was doing. Instead, I tried to keep all expression from my face and asked, "Why would she do that?"

"Because I'm a wild card and you're her little girl."

"I'm not that little," I muttered.

"You know what I mean. You'll always be her little girl, and all that other sappy stuff moms say to make you feel guilty."

"I liked it being just the two of us."

Gwen laughed. "You mean just the two of us and a handful of sunburned dancers, right?"

"It won't be the same if she's here."

"We can always pay some kid to fake an emergency and send her running back to the lodge occasionally."

I smiled. "Do you think your mom will come visit?"

It seemed like the perfect solution. Surely Grace would keep Mimi occupied and put any fears she had about Gwen's behaviour to rest. Gwen and I could go back to our own private routines.

Gwen snorted. "I know she won't."

"Why not? She's best friends with my mom, isn't she? She could stay for a weekend and they could keep each other company. Maybe she can come to one of your classes. Won't she want to see you?"

Gwen's shoulders stiffened and her face got hard. "Frankly I don't give a rat's ass what she wants. That was part of the deal."

"What deal?"

Gwen didn't have anything else to say on the matter, but I knew we were done for the day. Now both of us were firmly under the influence of our bad moods. She was practically crackling, she was so angry. I gathered up my shoes and slipped into the late afternoon without another word, heading to the beach to cool off. A dip in the lake would do me good.

But what kind of a deal had Gwen made with her mother, and what did it have to do with Sandy Shores?

* * *

That night Gwen didn't show up at dinner or campfire. I kept glancing at her window, expecting to see the hazy glow of her light behind the filmy curtain, but the room remained dark. There wasn't even a hint of movement. After Taps was sung, I asked Bo if he had seen Gwen.

"Nope."

"She wasn't at dinner."

"Nice catch, eagle eyes."

I frowned at him. "I'm worried about her. She hasn't missed campfire in ages."

Bo shrugged. "Technically she's off the clock. What she does after class is her own business."

"I'm going to check on her."

"Aw, leave her alone, Weenie."

"You make it sound like I'm bothering her. Why does everyone think I'm bothering her? Is it so hard to believe someone like her would enjoy my company?"

"Calm down, that's not what I meant. I just meant you should give her some space. Don't be so clingy."

"I'm *not* clingy—"

Bo cut me off. "Would you let me finish? You've been hanging off Gwen ever since she got here. Lay off for a bit. Everyone needs time to themselves."

His words stung. I turned on my heel and walked back to the lodge, trying not to think about what he'd said. But his words had buried themselves deep in my mind, like thorns. Did Gwen think I was clingy? Worse, had she actually said those things to Bo?

Despite Bo's advice, I stopped by Gwen's bedroom and locked lightly on the door.

"Gwen? Are you asleep?"

No one answered.

"I'm sorry if I upset you today by bringing up your mother. It's none of my business."

I listened carefully for a sign that she had heard me, or at the very least, that someone was alive in there: a snore, the squeal of a bedspring, the scritch-scratch of a pencil on paper, anything. I took a deep breath and spoke again. It was surprisingly easy to talk to a door.

"And I'm sorry if I've been hanging around too much. I just like having you here. But I can give you more space. I'm working in the office tomorrow, anyway, so you probably won't see me until dinner. Have a nice day."

Silence had never felt so empty.

* * *

That night I had trouble sleeping. My mind was like a record player and the needle was stuck, replaying my conversations with Bo and Gwen over and over again. I liked Gwen. I thought we were friends, but now I wasn't sure. Gwen listened and gave advice and did everything a friend should do, but I knew she was keeping things from me. What was the deal she had made with her mother? Why didn't she want her to visit? Who were the mysterious letters from? If we were really friends, she would feel comfortable confiding in me. I realized then that she was more like a big sister, one who gave advice and looked out for you, but never saw you as an equal.

DOII9

By Wednesday afternoon, the office was generally quiet. Most guests knew the Sandy Shores routines by then and had fewer questions, and there was usually still a day before next week's guests started calling with last minute questions. I spent most of the time reading, interrupted once when someone came looking for bait and a second time when a woman called to ask about the availability of groceries at Sandy Shores.

I tried not to think about the dance class I was missing, or the injustice that my mother had taken my place in it while I covered for her. Instead, I concentrated on my book, while sipping the extra-tall glass of lemonade I'd poured for myself as a treat. When the phone rang a second time, I grabbed the receiver without even closing my book.

"Good afternoon, Sandy Shores. This is Maureen Starr speaking."

"Well, hey there, Maureen Starr. I was wondering if you could connect me with a Gwendolyn Cates?"

It was a male voice, smooth and silky and somehow familiar.

"Who is this?" I asked, slipping a brochure between the pages of my book.

"Tell her it's Johnny."

Gwen had never mentioned a Johnny before. Still, how many people knew where she was?

"Are you a friend or a relative?"

Johnny laughed. "Something like that."

"I'm sorry, she's teaching right now. Maybe she can call you back?"

"See, that's the thing. I don't think she will. Do you ever get the feeling someone is avoiding you, Maureen Starr?"

I thought of the envelopes I delivered to Gwen, the ones with the postmarks from all over the place. Detroit. New York. Montreal. Toronto. They always had one thing in common, the name in the left-hand corner, G or possibly J something, the last name starting with S. All of a sudden I knew where I recognized the voice from. I was so shocked I almost dropped the telephone receiver. It was Johnny, as in *Johnny Skins*, the singer. I felt like I'd been struck by lightning.

"You're Johnny Skins."

"At your service."

"But you're—"

"Just a boy, looking to talk to his best girl. So what do you say, can you go get Dolly for me?"

"Dolly?"

"Dolly, as in Gwendolyn. You know who I mean. Can you just tell her Johnny wants to hear her voice? I'll even let her sing one of those sappy songs she's always ripping off some girlie singer."

"I'm sorry, I'm just surprised. She never said—"

"Aw, come on, you're telling me she never mentioned

me? Not even once? You're going to break my heart all over again."

"I thought she had a boyfriend, but she never mentioned his — I mean your — name."

"Sounds like you two have hung out some. How is she doing? Does she spend all day and all night crying over me, or has she moved on with some ruggedly handsome farmer? Or do you people fish up there? I can never remember."

"She teaches, mostly. Or stays in her room," I admitted. I didn't mention the bad mood his letters put her in, or how sad she seemed sometimes.

"I'm beginning to think she's forgotten all about me. I used to get two, three letters a week. Now I'm lucky if I get one. I'm worried someone else has caught her eye. Do you think you could go get her for me? I'd be forever grateful, Miss Starr."

I thought of Mimi, always lurking just out of earshot. "I don't think that's a good idea."

"What do you want, an autograph? Look, I'll sign a photo, just for you, and put it in the mail tomorrow. I've already got the address."

"It's not that, it's just not a good time."

"Ah, I see. The folks are around, right? Gwen mentioned something about a warden."

I tried to ignore that last comment. I wondered what else she had mentioned in her letters; more specifically, if she had mentioned me. I dismissed the thought almost as soon as it surfaced. Johnny would have recognized my name. She had kept me a secret, just like she had kept Johnny a secret from me. I thought of Gwen, bursting to the seams with all sorts of secrets, crying at night, trying to make the two halves of her life line up, when an idea dawned on me.

"We have these dances — they're parties, really — on Friday nights. Gwen runs them. The whole resort comes. Maybe you could just, turn up."

"A surprise visit?"

"Exactly! You could surprise her! She'd love that." I imagined the look of pure joy on Gwen's face when she saw her very own rock star on the beach at Sandy Shores. She would run into his arms and he would swing her around and say, "It was all because of Reenie."

Johnny paused. "I don't know. First you tell me I can't talk to her, now you're saying I should just show up? I feel like I'm being set up, here. What's in this for you?"

My mind was spinning with the possibilities. "Well, maybe you could perform. Just a few songs. People would love it."

Johnny laughed. "What are you, Maureen, some sort of opportunist?"

"Call me Reenie; everyone does. I'm not trying to make any money or anything, I just think it would be nice. Gwen's been working really hard and it would mean so much to have a real musician play at Sandy Shores, a famous one, just once. People would go crazy! Please?"

I had visions of the mess hall packed wall-to-wall with people, all of them screaming in surprise and delight as number-one hit-master Johnny Skins walked on stage. Not just Gwen, but Mimi would be thrilled — a private concert on her own property, miles away from any city. And Daddy could see how business-minded I could be. Everything seemed so perfect, any doubts I had disappeared and I knew I had to convince Johnny to come. If I could get him here, surely that would bring more people in and we'd never have empty rooms or cottages again.

"I don't know how you think these things work, Reenie, but I've got a manager, he books us gigs, real paying gigs. I'm pretty sure this would be a breach of something. I don't know what, but something."

"No one would have to know. You could say it just happened. You were coming up to see Gwen, and they pulled you on stage, and before you knew it—"

"All right, all right, I get the picture. Let me think about it. In the meantime, will you tell Dolly I called?"

"I will," I said, knowing full well I would never mention this phone call. I needed time to figure out how I was going to pull this off without anyone else knowing. I wanted to see the look on Gwen's face when Johnny Skins appeared out of thin air.

"Maybe we can arrange a time to talk, her and I. When is a good time?"

"Friday evening, around nine," I lied. "Everyone will be getting ready for campfire."

Johnny whistled. "Wow, sounds like a real wild place you're running up there. Do y'all hold hands and sing prayers, too?"

I ignored the dig. "Friday at nine?" I said.

"Friday it is."

"And think about the party," I added.

"I'm thinking about it right now," Johnny promised. "Bye, Reenie."

I hung up, my head spinning. Gwen was Johnny Skins' girlfriend. I wracked my brain, trying to recall everything I knew about him. I had seen him on the Ed Sullivan show just this past year. I could barely hear him over all the screaming girls in the studio audience. He was definitely one of the singers everyone whispered about at school, and

I knew for a fact Bo had at least one of his records.

I wanted to run over to the mess hall and search for his records, but Gwen would be there, teaching. I didn't want to arouse her suspicions, not yet. If I could get him to play at Sandy Shores, not only would Gwen and Mimi be thrilled, but the whole township would be excited. People would come from far and wide to see Johnny Skins play Sandy Shores, and I would be the one who made it all happen.

* * *

Knowing about Gwen's secret boyfriend made me look at her in a completely different light. Now she wasn't just Gwen, she was Dolly. Johnny Skins was not the kind of boy a mother wanted her daughter to go out with; he may have been handsome, but he was fast and reckless. It made Gwen seem dangerous, too. She had a whole other side to her that I had wondered about, but now I had proof. Gwen taught ballet to old ladies in a mess hall. Dolly was the tough girl-friend of a rock star. People wrote songs about girls like her. I watched her carefully and thought twice about her off-hand comments, wondering if she was referring to Johnny.

"Please stop staring at me; you're giving me the heebie-jeebies."

Apparently I wasn't as careful as I thought.

"I'm not staring," I lied.

"You are, too. If you're going to stare, you might as well make yourself useful. Watch this—"

Gwen slipped a record onto the turntable and ran to the front of the stage where she struck a pose — arms raised over her head, right hip cocked, face turned away — waiting for the lyrics to begin. She looked like a goddess on a Grecian urn, statuesque and still. I couldn't understand how someone

117

who was capable of dancing like Gwen could enjoy the kind of dancing that girl groups like The Shirelles did. Their moves were little and controlled — a shoulder roll here, a finger snap there — nothing like the shapes Gwen could make, sweeping across the floor, dancing with her whole body.

I watched her now, imagining two or three girls doing the exact same movements, wearing the exact same dress — something fitted and covered in sequins — with Gwen at the centre. She looked just like any other member of a girl group, confident and sophisticated. I clapped politely when she finished. She was very good, but it still seemed like a waste of her talent to me.

"I've done a little backup singing in some recording sessions," Gwen told me. I had heard this story before, but this time I was more interested. Now I wondered if she had done some backup for Johnny; maybe that was how they met.

"It's a good way to get my foot in the door. They like a girl who can move as well as she sings. At least *that* we know I can do."

"Do you know someone who could help you out? Someone in the industry maybe?"

Someone like Johnny, I thought.

Gwen shrugged the question off.

"I've got to get a demo recording together. I should have enough money saved up after this summer. God knows I'm not spending it out here. Maybe I'll even move to New York. That's where all the action is."

By action, did she mean Johnny?

"Can I pick a record?" I asked.

"Go ahead."

I found one of Johnny's albums, the one everyone knew, "Firecracker."

When the music started I watched Gwen carefully for a sigh, frown or secret look, anything that might give me a clue. She stretched out on her back, hands behind her head, eyes closed, chin nodding occasionally.

"Aren't you going to do a number to this one?"

"This isn't the kind of music that girls sing."

"What kind of music is it?"

"The kind that gets you into trouble."

Finally, now we were getting into Johnny territory.

"What kind of trouble?"

"The kind of trouble you can't even imagine."

Fine, so she wasn't going to divulge any deep secrets today. Not for the first time, I wondered why Gwen had agreed to come all the way to Sandy Shores if she hated the country so much. I knew it had something to do with her mother, but now I wondered if it also had something to do with Johnny. It couldn't be about the money, because I knew for a fact she was only making a few dollars a week. Daddy felt free room and board was more than generous for an employee who only worked a few hours a day, even if she was a professional.

When the song ended, she was quiet and seemed wistful.

It was now or never.

"I had an idea," I started. "But I'm going to need your help."

"What kind of idea?"

"You're always saying that there is never anything to do around here. So what if we gave people something to do? We could open up our Friday night dances to the whole county."

"That's not a bad idea. It would give kids a place to go. Listen to some good music, dance . . ."

"Exactly. I bet we'd get all sorts of people."

Gwen sprang to her feet and started pacing the length of the stage. "Reenie, you're a genius — I think it's a great idea. Now let's think bigger."

"What do you mean?"

"What if we had live music?"

This was working out better than I had hoped. Gwen had come up with the idea of live performances all on her own. I knew if we already had one or two musical acts, sneaking in a surprise performance from an honest-to-goodness rock-and-roll star would be even easier.

"How would we manage that?" I asked carefully.

"Easy. Put a notice up. You'd be surprised at all the musicians that crawl out of the woodwork. Your brother, for example. I bet his band would draw a crowd. Maybe I should work up a few numbers myself. It would be good practise."

"What do you know about Bo's band?" I asked.

"Please, the boy lives right above me. I could probably sing their entire set right now."

When Gwen was excited about something, not only did she laugh more, but she buzzed from idea to idea, totally transformed into someone bright and electric.

"We should pick a date in August to give us time to plan and book some performers," Gwen suggested. Then she squealed, adding, "I'm so excited! Let's go talk about this on the beach. I can't stand to be inside anymore."

The Plan

"So what's this I hear about a big party?" Bo said.

"Nothing," I said, struggling to keep the excitement out of my voice. "Gwen and I just thought it would be a good idea to, you know, bring the guests and the locals together. Just some live music, dancing . . ."

I trailed off and concentrated on the big bucket of peas Elsa had given me to shell for dinner. They were firm and waxy under my fingers, and they cracked open with a satisfying snap.

"Live music, huh?" Bo said.

"You know, bands and stuff. Do you know anyone who might be interested?"

Bo threw his head back and laughed. "You are a terrible actress," he said. There was a time when I would have been stung by a comment like that, but I was beginning to realize that being a good actress was like being a good liar, and I wasn't so sure I wanted to be either.

Bo sighed and sat on the step beside me, nudging my knee with his. "Come on, Reenie. If you've got something to say, just say it."

"Why, do you have someone in mind?"

"I do, actually. And I bet you do, too."

Bo dropped his hand into the bucket and scooped up a handful of bright green peas, shoving them all into his mouth at once.

"Hey! Those are for dinner!"

"No one will notice." Bo grinned, showing off the mashed up peas in his teeth. "Besides, Elsa loves me. Come on, Reenie. Spit it out. You know, if you ask me nicely I might say yes."

"What makes you think I want you to play?"

Bo grinned. "Come on. You and I both know that I am the best guitar player for miles around."

I sniffed. "I don't know that for sure."

Bo whistled. "When did you get so cold? I pity the poor sap who falls in love with you, Reenie."

"I didn't think you'd be interested in playing here. It's just an old mess hall, after all, at a lame family resort where nothing happens . . ."

Bo didn't take the bait. Instead, he slapped his thigh and said, "I'm in. Better yet, I'll get the boys to come, too. We'll all do it."

I set aside my peas and looked directly at Bo to make sure he wasn't pulling my leg. "Really? You'll do it?"

Bo took my hand and placed it over his heart. "Cross my heart and hope to die. Now let's talk about payment."

I took my hand back, shocked. "You want *money*?"

"We're your entertainment. You can't expect us to play for nothing."

"Will you play for food?"

Bo thought about it for a second.

"What kind of food?"

"Elsa's cooking."

Bo grinned and offered me his hand again, which I took. "Little sister, you've got a headlining band."

"I never said you would be headlining."

"Who else is going to do it?"

Now I was the one grinning. "You'll see."

* * *

When Friday came around, I lagged behind after dinner, claiming to have a stomach ache. Mimi put her palm to my forehead.

"Too much sun?" she asked.

I shrugged, acting as meek as possible. "Maybe," I lied. "Do you mind if I bow out tonight? I think I'm going to lie down."

"I can look after refreshments at the dance," Mimi said. "Scarlett, baby, do you mind doing the roasting sticks at campfire?"

"I'll do it," Gwen offered. "How hard can it be?"

Bo frowned. "It can get pretty messy. That marshmallow goo sticks to everything. Are you sure you can handle that?"

Gwen scowled. "You just don't want me to upstage you," she said.

Bo threw up his hands. "Fine. It's not like you do anything other than what you want to do anyway."

"You got that right," Gwen said, giving me a wink. "Feel better, Reenie."

I watched them go, feeling guilty. I wasn't used to lying. I kept reminding myself that I was doing this for Gwen and for Sandy Shores, but if I was going to be completely honest, I was doing it for myself, too. If I could make Gwen happy *and* save the resort, Mimi and Daddy would see me as an adult, someone they could trust, someone to be proud of.

True to my word, I spent an hour or so after dinner on my bed, but I was going over the plan in my head. No one so much as popped their head in to see how I was feeling. Once I was sure everyone was out, I crept down to the office to wait for my call in the near dark. When the phone rang, it was so loud I nearly knocked the receiver out of the cradle in my scramble to pick it up.

"Good evening, Sandy Shores. This is Maureen Starr speaking."

"Friday night at nine p.m. sharp. What did I tell you?"

"Hello, Johnny. Thanks for calling."

"So where's my best girl?"

"She had to work," I said, sticking to the line I had been going over and over in my head all day.

Johnny snorted. "Was there some sort of dance emergency?" he said.

I didn't know what to say.

There was a long pause that made my hands shake. Even far away, through a phone line, Johnny knew I was lying.

"Okay, Miss Starr, if you say so. But I gotta say, I feel like you're giving me a bit of a runaround here."

"No! She had to work, my parents insisted, I swear. Why would I lie to you?"

"That's just it. I can't figure out your game."

"No game — just a plan."

Johnny sighed long and loudly, like he was hard done by. "So, what's the plan?"

"Can you get up here in two weeks, on August tenth?"

"Well let me see . . ." Johnny trailed off. I imagined him checking a calendar filled with tour dates and interviews — until I heard him yell, "Bert! We got anything on the tenth?"

After a moment, Johnny came back on the line. "You sure

are lucky, Miss Starr. Something fell through and I am free as a bird on the tenth. Shall I get old Bert here to pencil you in?"

"So you'll do it? You'll really come?"

But Johnny was still in his own little world. "Lucky Miss Starr . . . I like the sound of that. Anyone ever written a song about you, Reenie?"

"No."

"They will, with a name like that. I bet you're cute as a button, too. I can tell by your voice."

I squirmed in my chair, feeling oddly disloyal to Gwen. "Do you need directions, or . . . ?" I left it at that, unsure of what else to say. Now that everything was confirmed, I just wanted to get off the phone. Johnny Skins might be Gwen's type, but something about him gave me the heebie-jeebies.

Johnny laughed. "No siree, I got someone to do that for me."

"Remember this is a secret," I reminded him. The last thing I needed was a big-mouthed rock star letting the cat out of the bag on some radio show. Or worse, on television.

"Heck, I'll probably forget all about it until old Bert here reads me my schedule. Isn't that right, Bert?"

"Who's Bert? Can he keep a secret?"

Johnny laughed. "Are you kidding? Bert is MISTER secret!"

He laughed again, and this time I forced myself to laugh along with him, though I wasn't exactly sure what was so funny. I wondered if Bert knew about Johnny and Gwen.

"Well, goodbye, then."

"You have a good night, Lucky Miss Starr."

I hung up and lay my forehead against the desk, drawing in a deep breath. My insides felt shaky and my head was spinning, but I was proud of myself. I had done it. Maybe Johnny was right — I was lucky. I hoped that luck wasn't about to run out. I would be needing more of it in the days to come.

The Right Kind of People

We had Bo's band secured, and my secret guest, now it was time to get the word out around town.

"We could make flyers," I suggested. "Hang them up around Orillia."

Gwen was doing leg lifts on the floor of the mess hall between classes. I lost count at forty-six, but that was at least five minutes ago. She barely broke a sweat.

"That sounds like the sort of thing old ladies do for a church function," she said. "You want to attract the right kind of people."

"What kind of people is that?" I asked, annoyed. So far it felt like I was the only one doing any work. All Gwen seemed to do was point out the flaws in my plans. This was supposed to be our project; there was something in it for both of us, after all. But lately Gwen had been preoccupied. She was never around when I went looking for her, and she wasn't as interested in hanging out and playing her records.

"Oh, you know, teenagers — cool people like you and me."

Gwen smiled before rolling over and starting her leg lifts on the other side. I was glad she couldn't see me blush.

"Right," I said. I may technically have been a teenager, but there was a world of difference between me and Gwen. I wondered if we met outside of Sandy Shores, would she think I was the right kind of person? Would she really think of inviting me, or would she just walk on by? The thought squirmed inside me like a worm in an apple.

Gwen started to speak, but most of her words got swallowed up by a yawn.

"Did you sleep okay?" I asked.

"Why do you ask?"

"You keep yawning."

Gwen smiled, waving me off. "Don't worry about me, Reenie. I'm not used to this gruelling summer schedule."

"You spend most of the time sunbathing or fixing people's posture," I pointed out. "That can't be more gruelling than ballet school."

"You're right. I haven't been sleeping well."

"Is it the bed? Maybe you can switch rooms."

"The room is fine. Really, Reenie, don't worry about it."

"It's Bo, isn't it? He's keeping you up. When he's not fiddling around on his stupid guitar, he's sneaking out at all hours of the night."

"No, that's not it," Gwen said quickly. "It's just this heat. So, where do people hang out around here?"

"It changes," I said, which wasn't a complete lie. But the truth was I had no idea. "The fairgrounds were popular for a while. People probably hang out at the Burger Palace now, too."

"Then all we need to do is let a few key people know about

it. They'll start talking, and soon everyone will know. So, step one, find out where the cool people are and let them know about the rockingest party they'll ever have the privilege of attending. Step two, show time!"

* * *

I felt heartened by my deal with Bo. He was still as elusive and mysterious as ever, but when he was around he seemed to smile more. Maybe all he'd wanted was for someone in the family to acknowledge that he was in a band and it mattered to him — even if that someone was his little sister who knew next to nothing about music.

"Did you ask the rest of the band?" I asked.

"Yup."

"And?"

"And they're cool with it."

"So you're in?"

Bo shoved my shoulder playfully. "I told you we were in. Don't look so worried. No one's going to back out at the last second."

"Tell them to invite anyone they want. The more, the merrier."

Bo's eyebrows inched into his hairline. "The more, the merrier?" he repeated. "What's that from, a nursery rhyme? I thought this was a rock 'n' roll concert."

"It is," I said, blushing furiously. Why couldn't Bo just let things slide?

"When people hear that Wide Mouth Bass is playing, you'll have to turn them away at the door."

"Wide Mouth Bass?"

"That's the name of our band."

"How do people know about you?"

A smile spread across Bo's face, the kind of smile that held a lot of secrets. I wondered just what kind of a following Wide Mouth Bass had. "Let's just say your event isn't the first gig we've ever played."

"I want to come next time."

"It's not really your scene."

"You don't know that," I protested, but Bo held up his hands.

"I don't think it's a good idea."

"You've been sneaking out for months and I haven't said a word, not to Mimi or Daddy."

"Reenie—"

"And I won't say anything, not if you promise to take me with you. Just once."

Bo shook his head, but I knew he would say yes. He didn't have a choice. It was bring me along or risk having his late night music sessions put to an end once and for all. It was a low-down, dirty thing to do, but I didn't have a choice. Both of us had a lot to lose.

"Fine. But don't say I didn't warn you."

"Good. So when's your next performance?"

Bo smacked his forehead, groaning. "Gig, Reenie. Actors perform. Musicians play gigs."

"You know what I mean. When's your next gig?"

"What are you doing tonight?"

"You mean—"

"We'll leave at eleven. Meet me by the Lookout. Make sure no one hears you."

"No problem," I said, sounding braver than I felt. "You're not the only one who knows how to sneak around this place."

PART THREE
FIRE
August, 1962

A Secret Weapon

Even campfire couldn't calm my nerves. I tried to focus on the flames, but they weren't having their usual calming effect. Part of me was impatient for campfire to be over, but I also wanted it to go on forever. I had no idea where Bo was taking me or what I was getting into, and I couldn't decide which was worse: the waiting or the not knowing.

Bo barely acknowledged me, as usual. He was relaxed and charming, and I envied his self-confidence. What would it be like to walk into a room or out onto a stage and perform without caring what people thought? Bo was wrong. Being a musician was a lot like being an actor, only you didn't have lines to hide behind. You were the one people listened to and came to see. It was performing the innermost parts of you. Being a musician was worse.

Once the singing had wound down, and Bo had played Taps, it was close to ten. I had an hour to get ready. I said a quick good night to Mimi and Daddy, careful to give them each a kiss, like I did every night. Then I hurried up to the lodge. Lately it seemed like everywhere I went, Mimi found a reason to show up. She continued to come to Gwen's classes

133

when she could steal away from the office, just as I had feared. When Gwen and I were relaxing on the beach, she would turn up, offering lemonade or a magazine. I didn't want to give her any reason to be suspicious, not while her antennae were already up. If I could just get to eleven o'clock without any questions, I was sure I'd breathe easier.

There was only one person I wanted to see. Gwen wasn't at campfire, but I looked up and saw that her window was open and the light was still on. I know she liked her privacy, but I needed a confidence boost even more. I knocked lightly on her door.

Gwen cracked it and peered out. She never once invited me in without first checking to see who it was, though I doubted anyone but me ever bothered coming to her room.

"Come in," she said, stepping aside to let me by. Her hair was wound up in a kerchief, and her face was hidden under a thick layer of cold cream. The room was hot and smelled strongly of nail polish. It made my eyes water.

"What's wrong with you?" she asked. "You're all jangly."

"I'm going to a party tonight," I admitted. "Bo's taking me."

"How did you manage that?" Gwen said with a smirk.

"I asked him."

Gwen crossed her arms, frowning at me. We both knew that wasn't exactly true.

"I asked him, and then I told him if he didn't take me I'd tell Mimi and Daddy what he's been up to at night."

Gwen laughed. "That's more like it: classic sibling blackmail. Don't worry about it, Reenie. You're just giving him a taste of his own medicine."

"That's not what I'm worried about."

"So what's the problem? Are you worried you'll get caught? Bo never has, and it's not like he's Mr. Careful, stomping all over that roof every night. It's amazing no one's figured it out. Except us, naturally."

I looked at my hands, embarrassed. "I'm nervous. What am I supposed to do? I don't even know where we're going."

"Relax. It's not like you'll be going to a secret underground nightclub. It's probably a bonfire in someone's backyard; someplace you've been a million times. Only this time there'll be booze and the boys of Wide Mouth Bass."

"You know the name of his band?" I asked.

Gwen shrugged. "Didn't you?" she asked.

"Do you want to come with us?" I asked, even though I knew I could never convince Bo to take both of us.

Gwen gave me a pointed look. "Do I look party-ready?" she asked, patting her covered head.

"How long would it take you to get ready?"

"Too long. Sorry, Reenie, as much as I'd love to cut loose with the country mice, I'm going to sit this one out. But before you go, I've got something for you."

I watched as Gwen leaned over her bed and dug through a pile of what looked like dirty laundry. She must have found was she was looking for, because she cried, "Ta-dah!" and the next thing I knew I was being smacked in the face by a piece of clothing. But not any piece of clothing; it was her red shorts.

"What's this?"

"Your secret weapon," Gwen said. "I guarantee if you walk into that party in those shorts, you'll have every single person begging to be on the guest list."

"I don't know, they're awfully—"

"Short? That's why they call them shorts, Reenie. Come on. You've got great legs. You should let them out once in a while."

"I was going to say red."

Gwen grinned. "The only thing better than short-shorts is red short-shorts. Now try them on."

"Turn around," I said.

Gwen rolled her eyes and flopped on the bed, throwing her arm over her face.

"Fine. I'm getting expensive cold cream all over my arm, all in the name of preserving your modesty. One year in dance school, Reenie, that's all you need. You'd be running around naked before you knew it."

I stepped out of my old shorts, which were permanently saggy and stained from a whole summer of campfires, and shimmied into Gwen's shorts. I wasn't convinced they would fit, but they slid over my hips and buttoned snugly against my waist. They felt sleek and glamorous, although I was shocked at how short they were. With my arms at my sides, there was at least an inch of bare skin between the tips of my fingers and the cuff of the shorts.

"I'm ready."

Gwen sat up and squealed. She was smiling so hard her face cream cracked over her cheeks like mud in the midday heat. "Perfect. Now all you need is your yellow blouse, the sleeveless one. But don't tuck it in. Leave a few buttons undone and then tie the ends up. I'd let you borrow my lipstick, but somehow I think you've reached your limit." Gwen sighed and swooned back against the pillows. "Oh, to be young and on the verge," she said wistfully.

Now I was the one rolling my eyes. "You're not even eighteen yet," I pointed out.

Gwen smiled sadly, like I was young and so naive and she knew better. "Sometimes I feel like I'm a hundred years old," she said. Then, with a sigh, "Have a good night,

Reenie. This old maid is going to get some beauty sleep."

I hated to see her like that, distracted and faraway. I wondered if she was thinking about Johnny. I noticed an envelope lying open on the pillow. It wasn't one of her mother's telltale cream ones, so it must have been from Johnny. Poor Gwen. Receiving letters from a loved one must be bittersweet. On one hand, it's nice to hear from them, but on the other it makes you miss them even more. Still, she had a boyfriend, a bona fide rock star, and was a beautiful dancer. A million girls would switch places with her in a second.

"You're hardly an old maid," I protested.

Gwen shook her head. "Trust me, sometimes it's better to be an old maid."

wide mouth bass

I heard my parents' door close at twenty to eleven, and Daddy started snoring moments later. The wind had picked up, rustling the leaves and toying with a loose tarp near the boathouse; it sounded like a flag, snapping in the wind. No one would hear me under all that night noise, which soothed my frayed nerves considerably. I lay fully dressed, perfectly still on my bed, imagining the people I might run into from school and what I would say to them. I figured if I had a couple of smart, snappy retorts ready, I could throw them out. Sort of like throwing treats at a strange dog, keeping it distracted so it didn't attack.

I kept craning my neck to look at the clock until it finally reached five to eleven. Then I sat up, smoothed Gwen's red shorts and slipped into the hallway. I was careful not to let the screen door slam and to stick to the trees lining the driveway.

Bo was waiting for me. When he smiled, his teeth gleamed. "You're early."

"So are you," I said evenly.

"Nice shorts."

I hoped he couldn't see my cheeks flaming in the darkness. "They're Gwen's."

"No kidding."

"So where are we—"

"Shh, not here. Follow me."

Bo turned and I followed him down the road. We walked single file toward the highway, one foot on the paved asphalt, still warm from baking in the sun all day, and one foot crunching in the gravel beside the ditch. Bo was wearing a loose T-shirt, sleeves rolled up over the thick part of his upper arms just like so many movie stars, his guitar slung over one shoulder. I wondered if girls thought he was a catch, if they came to see Wide Mouth Bass just to swoon over Bo Starr. The thought was so bizarre I almost giggled aloud. We left Sandy Shores property and were halfway to the gate at the end of the Simpsons' lane when a car suddenly sputtered to life, catching us in the glare of its headlights, bright and yellow as owl eyes.

"That's our ride," Bo said.

The passenger door popped open, and I heard someone say, "Isn't she a little young for you, Starr-man?" followed by hearty laughter.

"See what you're doing to my reputation?" Bo said, groaning, but he ushered me forward anyway. I ducked into the car and climbed across the front seat. A boy with big glasses and a T-shirt like Bo's was grinning wildly at me.

"Hello, sweetheart," he said, just like Groucho Marx. His thick eyebrows and oversized glasses made him look even more like Groucho. All he was missing was the cigar. I couldn't help but smile back at him.

Bo tossed his guitar in the back seat and then swung in beside me.

"Cut it out, Cracker. That's my sister," he said.

"Cracker?" I repeated.

"As in, Polly want a cracker," the boy said. "The name's Paul. What do they call you?"

"I'm Reenie," I said. "As in Maureen."

Paul slapped his thigh and crowed like a maniac. "Yee-ow! Bo you never told me your sister was a firecracker."

"She's not," Bo said. "Now drive. Let's get out of here before someone catches us."

"You're the boss, Starr-man."

As we drove to our secret destination, Paul talked non-stop. Bo cranked the radio to drown him out, but Paul just talked over the music. Sometimes he revved the engine, threatening to break all sorts of laws, but the speedometer barely edged past the speed limit.

The windows were open, and my ears were full of the sound of rushing wind and the bass that thrummed through the seats, jarring my bones. It was so exhilarating to be in the midst of all that noise that I completely forgot about being nervous.

Gwen was right; the party was in someone's backyard just outside Orillia. Paul pulled up and parked on what looked like someone's front lawn. I was about to protest that it didn't seem to be the kind of place you should be parking, but a dozen other cars were already there. The house was dark, but I could see a bright orange spot flickering near the barn, where a fire had been lit.

"Here we are, party people."

Paul crowed again and hopped out of the car. I scrambled after him as Bo retrieved his guitar from the back.

"Are you in the band?" I asked shyly, hoping it wasn't a stupid question.

"Sweetheart, I *am* the band," Paul said.

"What instrument do you play?"

"Nothing but the one God gave me," he said, pulling on a chain around his neck, kissing the cross that dangled there and pointing one finger skyward.

"Cracker here sings lead," Bo said, striding toward the bonfire.

I scrambled to keep up. "I thought you were the singer!"

Bo shook his head. "Backup, sometimes. I'm lead guitar."

"And songwriter," Paul added.

"We do half covers, half our own stuff," Bo clarified.

As we came closer to the bonfire, distinct shapes grew out of the darkness. There were a lot more people there than I had imagined. Some were sprawled across the hoods of cars pulled up on one side of the fire. Others were seated around the bonfire, and even more were standing in groups further off. It didn't look all that different from campfires at Sandy Shores, until you noticed that everyone there was young and no one was roasting marshmallows. Instead, they were laughing and chatting, cigarettes dangling from lazy fingers, the ends bright spots in the darkness. I'd thought they were fireflies until I got closer.

A few people looked over and nodded at us as we arrived. Some of the boys clapped Bo on the shoulder or cracked a joke at Paul's expense. He didn't seem to mind. Any attention was good attention for Paul. If anyone thought that it was strange to see me there, no one said anything. More than one person offered me a beer, but I declined each time. I didn't need beer — it was enough to be out here at my first field party. Besides, Bo would kill me.

One of the boys peeled away from a group and jogged toward us. "Finally, you're here. Jones is waiting for you.

You took your sweet time, didn't you?"

Paul shrugged. "You can't rush genius," he said.

The boy shook his head and laughed. "I hope you're not talking about yourself, Cracker." The boy's glance fell on me. He smiled and nodded in my direction. "Who's this?"

"My sister Reenie."

"Your sister, well, that explains it."

"Explains what?" I asked.

The boy punched Bo on the shoulder, grinning. "Bo here may be a rock star, but I never took him for a two-women kind of man."

I looked over at Bo, but he suddenly became very interested in his fingernails.

"What woman?" I asked.

The boy kept on grinning. He had a big smile, the kind that split his entire face in two.

"Same shorts, different girl."

"What does that mean?" I asked, but Bo was heading toward an old shed with Paul.

"Where are you going?" I called after him, hating the panic that slipped into my voice.

Bo kept going, calling casually over his shoulder, "To set up. Be good."

The boy laughed again. Laughter seemed to come so easy to him, like breathing.

"Are you going to let him boss you around like that?"

"He's even worse at home," I grumbled.

The boy rubbed his hair. It was thick and blond and looked like it had a mind of its own. Most boys either Brylcreemed their hair into submission or cut it short to the head, but not him. His was wild and full of life.

"Yeah, I know what you mean. I've got two older sisters."

Then he offered his hand. I shook it, feeling the warmth pass into my own skin. "I'm Ray."

"Reenie," I said.

Ray smiled. "Yeah, I know."

I recognized him from school. He was older, in Bo's year. He was long and tall and looked well scrubbed, even in the firelight. Normally an older boy would make me nervous, but Ray kept smiling at me. It was hard not to smile back.

"So are you musical, too?" he asked.

"No, not at all. I'm just an appreciator," I said, then instantly regretted it. What kind of word was "appreciator"?

"I'm an appreciator, too," Ray said. "Actually, I like to think of myself as a promoter." He gestured to the field. "I put these things together."

"This is your party?"

"Yep."

"Wow. There are so many people here."

Ray glanced around, smiling. "That has a lot to do with your brother's band. I just provide a time and a place."

I could see now why we hadn't been attracting outside crowds to our dances. Who wanted to do the bunny hop with their mother when they could be listening to live music in the middle of a field with no parents around?

"Do your parents know you're doing this?"

"My dad is cool with it. He knows something's up, but he doesn't sniff around too much. I guess he figures what he doesn't know can't hurt him. Or at least can't get him locked up."

My skin cooled instantly as visions of myself being driven home in the back of a police car, delivered in the middle of the night to a shocked Daddy and angry Mimi, took over my brain.

"Is this illegal?"

The smile slipped from Ray's face. "Hey, Reenie, I take this very seriously. I wouldn't do anything stupid. If someone gets out of hand, I get rid of them." He gestured to the party around him. "This is what I do: bring people together, show everyone a good time, let them know how good we have it around here."

Looking around, it was clear that promoting was something Ray was very good at.

"You know, I have something you may want to promote," I began.

"What's that?"

"I'm putting together a show at Sandy Shores in two weeks."

"What kind of show?"

"Live music, dancing, that sort of thing. Wide Mouth Bass is going to play, plus a few other surprise acts."

"What kind of surprise acts?"

I wanted to tell Ray, but I hesitated. If too many people found out, surely word would get back to Gwen and the surprise would be ruined. But without the draw of a big name like Johnny Skins, people might not turn up at all. While I was thinking it over, a murmur passed through the crowd. Ray touched my elbow. It was the smallest hint of a touch, but my skin tingled where his fingers had been.

"We'll talk about this later. I think the band is about to start."

I stood with Ray as Paul, Bo and two other boys took the stage. It was really just a patch of raked dirt in front of a rickety, old shed, and someone — Ray, maybe — had strung Christmas lights around its frame. The drummer sat on an overturned white bucket, the kind we used for bait. Still, the whole effect was magical.

As the boys took their positions, people started to move in closer, and soon I was standing shoulder to shoulder in a solid mass of people. Anticipation zoomed through the crowd like electricity. It was impossible not to feel charged up. Everyone was giddy and excited, and I had to rub my arms to make the fine little hairs calm down.

And then the music started.

At first I couldn't get over Bo, bent over his guitar like Elvis. He closed his eyes and threw his head around, shimmying his shoulders, kicking the dirt with the toe of his boot as if the crowd didn't exist. He was completely different from the charming and humble showman who entertained guests at our nightly campfires. Here he was something wilder, set loose.

Paul raced around, singing and clapping his hands and whipping the crowd up into a frenzy. Before, it had been hard to imagine anyone but Bo leading the band, but now I saw that he didn't have the same kind of crazy energy that Paul did. Paul was a pop bottle someone had shaken up then popped the top off of; he exploded over the stage in a burst of fizzy energy.

The songs were catchy, and I recognized most of them, thanks to Gwen's musical education. All around me people were nodding and singing along. I watched the crowd just as much as I watched the band, fascinated by their reaction. A group of girls clutched each other off to the side, gazing so longingly at the musicians that I felt embarrassed for them. One of them appeared to be sobbing into her friend's shoulder. Between songs, people clapped and cheered and called out requests. Paul taunted them, pretending not to hear, or making fun of their song choices, but in the end he always relented.

A few times I looked over and caught Ray looking at me. I blushed and looked away, pretending not to notice, but my heart was off to the races. I had never had a boy look at me like that, and a cute boy to boot. The crowd was so close that sometimes, as we swayed to the music, our arms touched.

By the end of the performance, I was hoarse from cheering and the back of my neck was damp with sweat. I was breathing hard, as if I had been the one running around on stage, but I felt like I could keep going all night. People begged and pleaded for more, and I joined in their chorus, but Paul dropped to the ground and played dead, not even moving when some joker pretended to kick him in the ribs.

Ray touched my shoulder and leaned down, speaking directly into my ear, "I'm going to go check on my rock stars. Will you wait here?"

"Sure," I said, every single inch of my body zinging. "Paul's my ride."

"Lucky Paul," Ray said before he jogged off to help the band pack up.

I watched him go, noticing how tall he was and how at ease in his body. Yet sometimes his shoulders crept up like he was nervous or bashful about something. It was endearing and brought a goofy smile to my face. I must have looked like some kind of simpleton, smiling at nothing, but I couldn't help myself. Gwen was always complaining about how men strung you out and made you feel old, but I felt like I was six years old and sitting in front of the biggest bowl of ice cream I'd seen in my entire life. With whipped cream.

"Reenie Starr?"

I turned and found myself face to face with Donna

Struthers from school. She was smiling at me, but there was nothing friendly about it. With her were Laura Jones, Mary-anne Black and Kitty Palister.

I faked a smile right back at her. "Donna! How are you?"

"I'm just fine, Reenie. Wow, I never thought I'd see *you* here."

Kitty sniggered, but I ignored her. I thought of Bo's performance and Ray's arm brushing mine, and I got such a rush of excitement that there wasn't any room for anxiety.

"Why should Bo have all the fun?" I said lightly.

"You look different," Donna said, walking forward to get a better look at me. I raised my chin and looked as bored as I could.

"Oh?"

"I love those shorts."

"Thanks."

It was now or never. Like it or not, I knew that if Donna Struthers was coming to a party, everyone would come. As mean as she was, she was one of the "right kind of people" Gwen was talking about. I needed her to get the word out.

"If you liked tonight's show, you should come to the party we're having in a couple of weeks."

"You're having a party?" Laura said. She smiled encour-agingly, and I wondered if maybe the two of us could be friends.

"You mean like those campfires your parents have?" Donna said, her voice dripping with condescension.

"No, more like a concert. Wide Mouth Bass is going to play, plus a few other acts." I had their attention now. I felt powerful. "And then there's the special guest . . ." I trailed off, enjoying the hungry looks on their faces.

Kitty narrowed her eyes. "What do you mean, special guest?" she asked.

"You've heard of Johnny Skins, right?"

Maryanne gasped and clasped Laura's hand. She looked genuinely excited. "Really? I love him!"

Kitty laughed. "You've got to be kidding. Johnny Skins would never play at Smelly Shores."

"Why not?" I said, ignoring the Smelly Shores bit. "He has to go on vacation sometime. Why not here? It's the perfect hideaway. No one would think to look for a rock star in Orillia, especially at a family resort."

Kitty rolled her eyes and turned to leave. "Come on, Donna, let's go. She's lying."

I returned Kitty's glare, not backing down even a little bit. "Fine. Don't come. You can hear about it secondhand. I just thought you'd want to know."

"Wait," Donna said, shaking off Kitty's hand. "I believe you."

Kitty looked shocked. "But, Donna—" she whined.

"Think about it. If he doesn't come, not only would everyone know what a liar she is, but she'd be a total laughingstock."

I shrugged, clenching my teeth so hard my jaw ached. "She's right," I said. "So are you coming? I wouldn't want you to miss out."

Just then, Ray appeared. I knew he was there before he spoke, because the hairs on the back of my neck stood up.

"Miss what?" he asked.

"The party at Sandy Shores," I said.

"The party I'm helping promote?" Ray asked.

"That's the one."

I wanted to take a picture of Donna and Kitty's faces so

I could remember this moment forever. It was shock incarnate. I couldn't wait to tell Gwen.

"So what about it, you ladies coming?" Ray asked, casually draping an arm around my shoulder.

Kitty managed to close her mouth, and Laura played with the end of her ponytail, giggling nervously. Only Donna was able to recover with any dignity.

"Sure, why not? Reenie and I go way back, don't we? I can't wait to see your family campsite in the summer," she said.

"Resort," Ray said, giving her a funny look. "It's a resort. I thought everyone knew that."

I could have kissed him right there.

* * *

It took a lot of effort to creep through the door and sneak up the stairs, when all I wanted to do was run and shout at the top of my lungs.

I paused at Gwen's door, listening for any signs that she might be awake. Bo frowned and pointed at my bedroom, mouthing "tomorrow." But it was past two in the morning — it already was tomorrow! I had never been up this late in my life. I wanted the sun to come up and the day to be here so I could tell Gwen all about my night. I wanted to comb through her records and find the songs that captured what was going on in my heart and my head.

I paused in my doorway, wanting to thank Bo, but what could I possibly say? All I could do was keep on grinning that same goofy grin, the one I had never smiled until this night. It was like Ray had pulled an entirely new smile from inside me. It was a Ray smile. The thought was so ridiculous, and so true, that it made me smile even harder. My cheeks were beginning to hurt. Bo rolled his eyes.

"Don't think this is going to be a habit. It was a one-time thing," he muttered, heading toward the stairs.

I didn't answer; I just continued smiling.

If he wouldn't take me, I'd find a way.

secrets and lies

I managed to get some rest, but sleep or no sleep I was bright and full of energy come morning.

At breakfast, I ate quickly and carefully, watching for signs that Mimi suspected anything about my nighttime adventures. But she just chattered about the party and whether or not she needed a new dress.

"What about me, do I need a new dress?" Scarlett piped up.

"You have so many pretty ones, sweet pea, but maybe a haircut." She reached out and twirled a section of Scarlett's hair, almost white from the sun, around her finger. "I swear your hair grows an inch a day."

"Has anyone seen Gwen this morning?" I interrupted.

"It's only eight o'clock. How often do we see her before ten?" Mimi said.

"I'm going to wait for her in the studio."

"Brush your teeth first!" Mimi called.

I rinsed the orange juice out of my mouth with a glass of water and ran all the way to the studio, breathing in the deep, spicy scent of the pine trees and wondering if anything had ever smelled so sweet.

"Well, well, well, you're awfully chipper this morning!" Daddy smiled at me. He was on his way to the dock, a fishing rod in one hand and his old tackle box in the other. "I'm going fishing. Want to keep me company? You can tell me what's got you smiling so big."

I barely stopped, calling over my shoulder, "No thanks, Daddy! I'm meeting Gwen for a lesson!"

There was a time when all I wanted to do was go fishing with my dad, but today I had too much on my mind. I couldn't wait to talk to Gwen about last night.

"You two are certainly getting along."

"Yep! Like a house on fire," I said, using one of his own corny sayings. "'Bye, Daddy!"

I knew it would be a while before Gwen made an appearance, but I was so wound up that I swept the entire mess hall, dusted the record player and flung open all the windows to let in the sweet smelling breeze. I found the album I was looking for and played "Maybe" by The Chantels over and over again, carefully moving the needle and then dropping it back into the right groove. I felt a little crazy, but it was a wonderful kind of crazy, like I was a top that someone had set spinning across a table.

"It is too early in the morning for that," Gwen said. She was standing in the doorway, hand on her hip, hugging a steaming mug of coffee to her chest, but she was smiling. "I take it everything went well?"

"It went better than well!"

Gwen hoisted herself onto the stage and sat beside me. "Go on, then. You've got something to spill, so spill. But first, can we please change the record? You've played that sappy song enough times for one morning."

"You heard?"

Gwen rolled her eyes. "The whole resort heard."

"I don't care!" I said recklessly.

Gwen squinted at me. "Is this about a boy?" she asked.

"How did you know?"

Gwen sighed. "Now you *really* have to tell me everything."

I started with meeting Ray and ended with us standing together, staring down Donna. I left out the part where I happened to tell Donna that Johnny Skins would be making an appearance.

"You should have seen the look on her face," I gushed. "I can honestly say I've never wanted to kiss a boy before, but now . . ."

Gwen shook her head. "I never should have let you wear those shorts."

I laughed, but it was short lived. One quick look at Gwen's face and I realized she wasn't joking.

"Why? This is a good thing."

"It always feels like a good thing in the beginning, but then it gets . . . complicated."

"I thought you would be excited for me."

"I am. I just think you should take it easy, be careful. Look before you leap, you know?"

Irritation prickled my skin like heat rash. "All I said was I met a boy. I didn't say I was in love."

Gwen tried to pinch my cheek, but I dodged her hand, scooting further away from her.

"Look at you," she said sadly. "I know a smitten kitten when I see one. Take it from someone who's been there. Right now he's all you can think about. You feel invincible, like you could jump off a building and land on your feet.

But soon all you'll be thinking is, why didn't he call? And when he does call, he'll be so aloof it'll drive you crazy. The next thing you know, you're fighting again. It's a vicious, vicious cycle."

Gwen was looking at me like I was just a dumb kid, but I knew plenty. I was sick of people telling me all about life, and the things I should and shouldn't do. Wear these shorts, listen to this music. She looked so smug, lounging in my mess hall, in my resort, giving me advice about someone she had never met. This wasn't about me, it was about her. And so I called her on it.

"Ray's not Johnny."

"What?"

"I know about you and Johnny Skins. He's the one who writes you those letters. He's the one you've been crying over."

Gwen's face hardened. She pulled herself up to her full height, hands on her hips. "I didn't take you for the type to go through someone else's mail," she said, practically spitting the words at me.

I flinched. "I didn't go through your mail. I delivered it. And he called one day and I was in the office."

Gwen paled. "He called here?"

"You were teaching a class," I said weakly. "I was going to tell you, but—"

"He shouldn't be calling here."

"I didn't tell anybody."

"Good."

Gwen started pacing. It made me nervous, so I added, "I can keep a secret," just to calm her down.

Gwen laughed, but it sounded more like a bark. "It's not that," she said, throwing her hands in the air. "Everyone knows. There was even a picture of us in the paper once, backstage after a show. Only they didn't print my name. I was just another nameless backup dancer. Why do you think my mother sent me here?"

Gwen's voice was so bitter it made me cringe. I felt like I was the one keeping her here. Suddenly it all made sense: the crying, the letters, the homesickness. This was more than Gwen just missing her boyfriend; she was being kept from him. No wonder she hated being here so much. Mimi and Gwen's own mother were conspiring to keep them apart. I couldn't believe that Mimi, of all people, would agree to such an arrangement. Gwen was in love with a rock'n'roll star and was forbidden to see him. I couldn't imagine anything more dramatic, more glamorous.

"I didn't know," I breathed.

"Of course you didn't! You weren't supposed to know. I was supposed to forget all about him. Now what am I supposed to do?"

"Gwen, I swear I won't tell. No one here knows; I didn't tell anyone about the phone call."

Or the deal I'd made, I thought. Bringing Johnny up here was supposed to be a nice surprise for Gwen, something to cheer her up. But now I wondered if maybe I had been too hasty in inviting him.

"What did he say?" she demanded.

"Nothing," I said carefully. "He wanted to talk to you and I said you were teaching."

Gwen sighed. "I guess that's not so bad," she said.

People started to filter through the back door. Gwen rubbed her eyes with her fists. It was a gesture I had seen Scarlett do a million times when she was sleepy or upset. Watching Gwen do the same thing was unsettling. For one horrible moment I wondered if she was going to cry.

Instead, she took a deep breath, thrust her shoulders back and took charge. "Find me something to warm up to," she ordered.

* * *

Dance classes were cancelled Thursday and Friday because the mess hall was decorated and Gwen wanted time to rehearse. This was a wrinkle I hadn't planned on. With Gwen out of the studio and lounging around the resort, it would be much harder to sneak Johnny in without her knowing.

As previously arranged, I went into the office on Thursday just before three to wait for his phone call. I told Mimi that I would watch over the office for the rest of the day if she'd like a break. Mimi was so pleasantly surprised that I felt guilty.

"Aren't you sweet?" she said. "You are the sweetest of my children."

"That's not true," I demurred. "Scarlett is the sweetest."

"Only by virtue of her age," Mimi said, tapping my left cheek right where it dimpled. I smiled and her finger sank into the dimple and she tickled it, took out her finger and flicked imaginary dust into the air, just like she used to do when I was little.

"Look at all that stardust," she said.

I rubbed my cheek, half embarrassed, half pleased. She hadn't done that in ages.

Then, Mimi took both shoulders in her hands, bent over and searched my eyes. "How are you, Reenie? Are you okay?"

I blushed under such close scrutiny. "I'm okay."

"I'm not sure I believe you."

I didn't know what had brought on Mimi's burst of

SUMMER DAYS, STARRY NIGHTS

concern, but it was getting close to three and I was worried Johnny would call at any second.

"I'm fine. I've just been busy."

Mimi frowned. "Busy with Gwen, not busy with girls your own age. Is there anyone you want to invite on Friday? Some girls from your class? You spend too much time around here. You need to get out, enjoy life."

"I do enjoy life," I protested.

"I know, sweet pea. I just meant with girls your own age."

When I didn't answer, she went on. "Maybe I'll just stay here and we can have a little girl talk. We haven't done that in ages. Look at you, a half-grown woman. Pretty soon, I'm not going to recognize you."

Mimi ran her finger down the top of my head, re-parting my hair. I brushed her hand away. This was not the time for her to be playing the doting mother.

"I don't feel like talking, Mimi. I just want to read my book. I thought you could use the break, but if you'd rather stay here, I guess I could go read by the lake."

Mimi pouted. "Fine. I know when I'm not wanted. I'll leave you to your dry old pages and I'll go have fun elsewhere."

She sashayed out of the office, smiling and wiggling her fingers at me as she left, letting me know it was all an act, and she wasn't mad. But I wondered if maybe I should have let her stay. Mimi's bouts of affection were brief and few and far between. More often than not they were directed at Daddy or Scarlett, who lavished in the attention like a cat in the sun. Although there was no doubt in my mind that Mimi loved Bo and me, she was careful with us and kept her distance. It was like she knew we didn't trust her.

Mimi was just out of sight when the phone rang. I picked it up on the first ring.

"Good afternoon, Sandy Shores. This is Maureen Starr speaking."

"Reenie, Reenie Starr. Did anyone tell you your name is like a song?"

"Mr. Skins? Is that you?"

I heard a laugh. "Mr. Skins? That sounds just plain wrong. I told you to call me Johnny."

I breathed a sigh of relief. "Thank goodness it's you."

"Isn't that nice to hear. Most hotels hate hearing from me."

"We're not a hotel, we're a resort."

"I know, I know. No room service, no bellhops, none of that star treatment. Well that's just fine with me. To tell you the truth, I'm getting sick of the whole game. I need to reconnect with the people, you know? Do something real."

"But you're still going to play on Friday, right?"

"Of course I am! Don't you worry your pretty little head, Reenie Starr. Johnny doesn't go back on his word. Now how's our girl doing?"

"Gwen? She's fine. She's down by the lake right now."

"I'll bet she's a sight for sore eyes. You still keeping her in the dark?"

"She has no idea."

"That girl's going to get the surprise of her life. So what's the plan?"

"I've booked you a room under the name John Smith."

Johnny laughed. "John Smith? That's a little . . . obvious, don't you think?"

I bristled a little. "I think it's just right. Can you be here by four o'clock on Friday?"

"You're the boss."

"I'll be in the office to check you in. I'll take you directly to your room. You can't be seen until the party."

"What about my band?"

"What band?"

"I have to bring my boys with me. I'm not a one-man road show."

I gritted my teeth and glanced at the guest register. We were almost full.

"How many people is that?"

"There are four of us."

One person I could hide away in the lodge, but four was going to be hard to explain. Somehow I knew they wouldn't settle for rooming together, or even in pairs. All I could hope for was that Mimi and Daddy would be so distracted by the party, they wouldn't notice a few extra bodies.

"I'll see what I can do."

"So let me get this straight. We're going to drive up, check in with you at four, hide away until you come knocking, then blow all the country folk right out of the water with some tunes."

"Right."

"When do I see my Dolly?"

"At the party," I said. "She's hosting."

"And after?"

"You can catch up after."

Johnny broke out into more laughter. "'Catch up.' Is that what you kids are calling it up there? Well, Gwen and I sure have some catching up to do."

I was glad he couldn't see me blush. This was the third time I had spoken with Johnny Skins, and I still couldn't understand what Gwen saw in him. I knew from his television appearances that he was handsome and a talented singer, but surely manners had to count for something? I thought of Ray and his non-stop smile and how kind he had been. I wondered what he was doing right now, and if he was thinking of me.

"You still there, Reenie Starr?"

"Yes."

"So everything's A-OK then?"

"I think so."

"We'll roll up around four, then."

"Sounds good. And Johnny, if you don't mind, could you show up dressed like you're about to spend the week fishing? I don't want to draw any attention."

"Are you afraid I'll show up in my leather jacket and jeans?"

"It's just that your performance is supposed to be a surprise, and if you show up looking like, well, you know . . ."

"Don't worry, kiddo, I hear ya loud and clear. I'll get myself a boring shirt and some old man sunglasses. See you tomorrow."

I hung up and penciled three more fake names into the lodgings list, hoping no one would notice or ask me about it. In my head I ran over all of the things I had to do before Friday: make up the rooms, sneak in the band, grab them food, keep Gwen distracted and away from the lodge as much as possible, pick an outfit. I was exhausted and exhilarated at the same time. I felt like I could burst into tears or run all the way to Orillia. Surely a person couldn't take any more excitement? When the phone rang again, I pounced on it.

"Good afternoon, Sandy Shores. This is Maureen Starr speaking."

"Reenie?"

"Yes. Who is this?"

"I thought it was you, but you sound different on the phone, very professional. It's Ray."

My heart leapt to my throat. I had to swallow before I could answer. "Hi, Ray. How did you get this number?"

"It's the Sandy Shores number. I was hoping you, or maybe Bo, would pick up. Otherwise I'd have to ask your dad to speak with you. Which I would do, by the way."

I smiled, wondering if Ray could tell, if it was possible to hear a smile in someone's voice.

"Right, of course. How are you?"

"Great! I'm just calling to check on our party situation. Is there anything you need me to do?"

"Just make sure people know about it, convince them it's going to be a great party."

"Sure, although the word is out and it sounds like people are excited. I've even heard a few crazy rumours."

I swallowed. "Oh?"

"But that's a good thing. It doesn't matter if it turns out to be true, rumours get people interested. It's going to be a great party, Reenie. It's about time those boys got a real gig."

"Thanks. I hope you're right."

"Are you bringing anyone?"

I held the receiver away from me, just in case Ray could hear how loudly my heart was thumping. "To the party? No. Why?"

"Good. I wanted to ask you to dance, but it would have been awkward if you were there with someone else."

"No, no one. It'll be just me."

"Not anymore," said Ray. "Now it'll be you and me."

I was wrong. A person can definitely be even more excited.

JOHNNY SKINS

Luckily, Friday was a beautiful day — hot and sunny, with barely a trace of humidity. Everyone was at the beach or on the lake, making the most of their last full day at Sandy Shores. Daddy had gone fishing and wouldn't be back until five at the earliest. I offered to staff the office while Mimi took a nap.

"What a dear," she said. "I'm going to lie down. I can feel a headache coming on."

I had never been so glad to see Mimi disappear up the stairs to her room. With a bit of luck she would be out for hours and wouldn't hear me sneak Johnny and his band into the lodge. I couldn't find Bo anywhere, which wasn't a surprise, but I worried about him turning up out of nowhere just as Johnny's car pulled in. Gwen was in the mess hall, practising for her debut solo performance.

"Tonight is the real deal," she had told me at lunch. "No backup singers, no showy dance moves, just me, myself and I."

It was odd to see her so nervous. She talked a lot and fidgeted with her hair, which had grown out and looked almost girlish curling over the nape of her neck. Without her red lips she looked five years younger. She didn't look like she'd walked off the silver screen anymore, but somehow she looked prettier, more like the Gwendolyn I'd met years ago. Sandy Shores had worn off her sheen, and now I could look at her and see a real person, instead of the pin-up girl she pretended to be.

Hopefully she would be tied up practising until I could get Johnny and his band safely indoors.

My stomach clenched at the sight of every car that drove by. Maybe it was my imagination, but I felt like more cars than usual were passing by. Sandy Shores was located on a side road; it was not the kind of place people cruised past unless they were looking for it.

To make matters worse, the phone was ringing off the hook. People were calling up, asking about the party tonight: who was going to be there, how much did it cost, where could they park? I was as helpful as I could be, given my jangling nerves, reassuring people that it was bound to be a great night. But in my head, I was worrying about all the things that could go wrong. What if Johnny didn't show up? What if we ran out of food? What if we didn't have enough space? The what-ifs were eating me up from the inside out. My stomach was knotted so badly I couldn't even look at food, let alone eat it.

Finally, forty-three minutes later than we had discussed, a big blue car nosed itself into the driveway, followed by an old van. I ran to the window to get a better look. Sure enough, there was a group of men packed into that boat of a vehicle. Now that they were here, a whole new set of what-ifs attacked. What if we're seen? What if they make a mess of their rooms? What if they don't like the sandwiches I made them? I tried to think like Daddy, the consummate businessman and host, and dashed out to meet them.

"Hello there!" I called, trying to catch my breath as the last one extracted himself from the car. Four young men stood awkwardly in the sunshine, dressed in jeans and T-shirts, their hair so full of Brylcreem that it shone. So much for them coming in disguise. Two of them opened the back of the van and started unloading equipment. A fifth young man, about the same age but wearing a jacket, came right up to me and offered his hand.

"Maureen Starr? I'm Bert Fontaine."

So this was Bert. Bert didn't look much older than the other guys — the band members, I guessed — but he was the only one who had shaved and put on something fancier than a T-shirt. His shirt had a starched collar and looked clean, which was more than I could say for the other guys. They looked like a group of moody old crows, in their black jeans and hunched shoulders, glowering into the sunshine. Only one of them looked pleased to be there. He came forward as I shook Bert's hand.

"Lucky Miss Starr, we finally meet." Johnny Skins was shorter than I expected, and much slimmer. In fact, he was the smallest member of the band. He was handsome, but he had a grin that meant trouble. There was nothing kind or genuine in it. Regardless, he was a guest and he was doing me a favour. I took his hand and shook it. Before I had a chance to pull back, Johnny dipped low and kissed my hand.

"I was right. You are as cute as a button."

Bert cut in as I pulled my hand away. "Miss Starr, do you think you could show us to the boys' lodgings? We've been in the car a long time and they need to rest up and eat something before the show."

"Of course, right this way."

I was only too happy to get them out of broad daylight and into the lodge. I offered to carry a bag or two, but Johnny laughed.

"What kind of gentleman lets a lady carry his load? Right, fellas?"

The other band members mumbled a reply. None of them had taken off their sunglasses. It was hard to read their expressions, let alone tell them apart. They hadn't even bothered to introduce themselves to me. So far, I was unimpressed. Was this really the world Gwen and Bo so desperately wanted to be a part of?

"How about this sun?" Johnny said, lifting his arms and face to the sky. He took off his sunglasses and crowed, "Hallelujah!" at the top of his lungs.

I glanced across the road and saw that people were starting to gather up their beach things. As far as I could tell, no one had seen us. Sandy Shores was full of the sounds of kids shouting and playing, but the members of a rock and roll band wouldn't go unnoticed for long. Dinner would be served in less than an hour and some guests would be making their way to the lodge. We had to get out of sight and fast.

* * *

"And here's where you will be staying, compliments of Sandy Shores."

I opened the door and ushered Johnny into his own private room, which was as far away from the dining hall and the mess hall as possible. I had already dropped off the other band members in their rooms across the way. They barely acknowledged me, just grunted their thanks. I had only made up four rooms, but Bert swore he didn't mind sharing.

I watched as Johnny strode through the room, running

a hand over surfaces and looking in drawers. He was making me nervous. What was he looking for, I wondered. I had never been in a city hotel, but I couldn't imagine their rooms were any nicer than ours. I had spent all morning sprucing things up, changing the linens, dusting the furniture and stocking the rooms with bottles of Coca Cola and sandwiches I had made myself and wrapped in wax paper.

"You sure are a little professional, Lucky Starr," said Johnny.

"Thank you," I said, unsure of whether or not I was being complimented.

Johnny sat on the bed, kicked off his shoes, crossed his feet, and pulled a squashed cigarette pack out of his sleeve.

"There are sandwiches on the table there, and some pops. Can I get you anything else?" I asked.

"Pretty little place you got here," Johnny said, ignoring my question. "I guess this is what they call quaint."

"Thanks."

"Bet you can't wait to get out of here."

"Not really."

Johnny looked surprised. I didn't mean to sound brusque, but he was getting on my nerves. I hated the way he lazed about, not a single grateful bone in his skinny body. I was trying to picture him with Gwen, but I couldn't see them talking or dancing or getting along.

"You don't want to head south, check out the big city? There is lots of opportunity for a pretty thing like you." Johnny winked. "I bet you're smart, too."

Johnny lit a cigarette. I wrinkled my nose. Within seconds, the lovely lemon scent of the cleaning oil I'd used disappeared under the ashy, burning smell of the cigarette.

"Is there anything else I can do for you before I go?" I asked again.

"Yes. When do I see my Dolly?"

"After the concert," I stalled. "She's busy rehearsing now."

"Planning to shake her stuff for the old fogies, is she?" Johnny flicked the end of his cigarette on the edge of the bedside table.

"There's an ashtray in the drawer," I said.

Johnny nodded but continue to tap his ashes on the table. A little pile of papery grey flakes smouldered against the wood. I felt about as steamed up as those ashes.

"No, she's singing."

Johnny gave a long, world-weary sigh. "Still chasing that old dream, is she?"

"You don't think she's a good singer?" I asked, surprised. Surely a boyfriend, or a good one, would stand behind his girlfriend and her dreams.

"Sure she is, but girl singers are a dime a dozen these days. That girl is an ace dancer. She should stick with what she's good at. I don't need a girl to sing backup. But a good-looking dancer?" Johnny grinned. "That I can always use."

Something didn't feel right. All of Gwen's plans involved recording a demo and landing gigs. I couldn't imagine she'd be happy hanging around in the background, dancing at Johnny's shows, even if he was her boyfriend.

"She tours with you?" I asked.

"That's the plan. It's nice having your girl around. You got a boyfriend, Lucky Starr?"

"No."

"Don't worry. You will. And then you'll know. You'll want to be with him all the time. This summer has been hard on me. I miss having my Dolly around. You sure you can't sneak her up here for one little second?"

"I'm sorry, but she's rehearsing."

Johnny snorted. "Who did she convince to sing with her? A couple of choir girls?"

"My brother is accompanying her on guitar."

Johnny took a long drag on his cigarette, never taking his eyes off me. They were not friendly eyes, like Ray's, which had seemed to dance in the firelight. Johnny's eyes were cold and hard as stones. "Your brother?"

"Yes, Bo. He plays guitar in his own band, Wide Mouth Bass. They're playing tonight, too. You'll get to meet him. He'll be thrilled."

"What kind of a name is Bo?"

I bristled. "It's short for Bogart."

"This brother of yours, does he have a girl of his own?"

"I don't know," I said honestly. "He never tells me anything."

Johnny smiled. "Isn't that just like an older brother? Well then, Lucky Starr, if you're not going to bring me my Dolly—"

"I'm sorry, but she's—"

"Rehearsing. Yes, I know. And I doubt you're going to bring me a beer . . ."

I hesitated. "I really shouldn't."

Johnny shrugged. "No harm in asking. I'll see you later tonight."

"I'll come get you when it's time," I promised.

"Don't be too long," Johnny said, making puppy dog eyes. "I get lonely real quick."

"See you soon," I said, closing the door firmly behind me. I shuddered — I wanted to get as far away from Johnny Skins as possible. Before, all I could think about was what I would do if Johnny didn't show. Now, all I could think about was how soon he could leave.

Showtime

People started coming as early as seven o'clock. Daddy was in charge of directing traffic and showing people where they could park. I went over to the front lawn to see if he needed anything and also to remind him when things were starting. He was still wearing his fishing hat and his arms were red from too much sun.

Daddy shook his head in disbelief. "Would you look at all these cars!" he said.

"They're coming to see Bo play," I said. "Pretty impressive, huh?"

Daddy agreed. "You can say that again. It's like Canada Day."

"Bigger," I pointed out. "Are you going to be able to see the show?"

Daddy busied himself with a couple of tough old dandelions that had escaped his wrath earlier in the summer. He didn't look up at me when he answered.

"We'll see, Reenie. I thought I might hang out here to watch over the cars. We don't want any kids thinking they can sneak away and get into trouble when no one's looking."

"Okay," I said lightly. I didn't want to push him. Daddy wasn't as thrilled about the concert as the rest of the Starrs. He stayed quiet when we discussed it at dinners. A little part of me felt bad about not asking him in the first place, but he had put Mimi in charge of entertainment, and he seemed to be spending more time than ever on the lake this year. I'd hoped he would come see Bo, and maybe he'd realize how much music meant to him. But that wasn't looking likely.

"You better get back there," Daddy said. "It's coming on close to eight o'clock."

I rushed back to the mess hall. I felt like I had been rushing all day. I was all amped up, like someone had replaced my heart with a crank engine and the arm was spinning out of control. I didn't have time to breathe, let alone eat. I told myself I could do all that tomorrow.

Outside the mess hall, Mimi had set up a card table and was taking admission. She was chatting with a few ladies as I arrived.

"A young man named Ray was looking for you," she said, a twinkle in her eye. "A handsome young man, I might add."

The other women exchanged glances, but I slipped into the mess hall before they could tease me. Looking down at my old shorts and the blouse I had been wearing all day, I regretted not leaving myself time to change into something nicer. The whole town had dressed up, and I looked like I had spent the day fishing. I tied up the ends of my blouse like Gwen had shown me and shook out my hair, smoothing all the loose strands back into a ponytail. That would have to do.

I knew the mess hall would be packed, but when I stepped inside, the sight of all those people took my breath away. I'd thought our Friday night dances were successful, but the most we'd ever had to one of those was thirty-six people. There looked to be five times that number in here now.

Someone had removed most of the chairs to make more room, leaving two rows along the back for the older guests who sat there, fanning themselves and holding cold bottles of pop to their foreheads to cool down. It was unbearably hot, but people seemed happy, standing around with their friends, chatting and dancing on the spot to our pre-show music. I looked to see if someone had shut the windows, but they were all open. Whatever breeze there was didn't stand a chance against all those bodies.

I was anxious to get the show on the road. I searched the room for Gwen, but she was nowhere to be seen. Deciding she must be out back with the band, I took a determined breath and headed toward the back door by the stage. I excused myself as I squeezed past the guests, and kept an eye out for Ray.

I had set up a tent just outside the mess hall for the performers. Gwen had told me most performance spaces have a "green room" where the musicians wait for their turn to perform. When I'd shown her the makeshift tent, filled with cushions to sit on and Thermoses of lemonade, she said, "It's not exactly a green room, but it'll do."

The boys of Wide Mouth Bass didn't seem to mind. When I came in looking for Gwen, I found them having a great time challenging each other to lemonade-chugging contests. Gwen wasn't there, but Ray was with them. My stomach turned inside out at the sight of him. He was sitting on the floor of the tent, arms resting on his long legs, his big smile warming the whole place up.

"Stop that!" I said, making a grab for the lemonade. "We need to save some for the others."

"What others?" Cracker asked, wiping his mouth with the bottom of his shirt. "C'mon, Reenie! I'm dying to know who we're opening for. Can you give me just one little hint?" He wiggled his bushy eyebrows at me and I laughed, but still refused to divulge any information.

"She won't even tell me and I'm co-promoter," Ray said.

"Bang-up job as always, Ray-baby," Cracker said, peeking through the back door. "That's a great crowd."

"Who's out there?" Bo asked.

I joined Cracker at the door and looked out at the crowds. It was mostly young people, but there were quite a few families, some older people from town and all of our Sandy Shores guests. "Tons of people," I assured him.

"Has anyone seen Gwen?" I asked.

"She's getting ready," Ray explained. "She said to start without her."

I couldn't imagine starting without Gwen. This was our project, we had worked on it together.

"She won't mind. You know how she is," Bo said, rolling his eyes. "She wants to look perfect."

Wide Mouth Bass was on first; Gwen wouldn't be singing until later. She had lots of time to get back before it was her turn to go on.

"Okay, fine. Ready?"

Cracker cheered. "This is it. Are you ready, boys?"

The other band members yelled back at him. I watched as they formed a close huddle, heads together, chanting something that didn't even sound like English. I met Ray's eyes across the huddle.

"What are they doing?" I asked.

Ray shrugged, grinning. "It's a pre-show ritual, something bands do to get them in the mood."

"What language is that?"

"English, sort of. Cracker wrote this motto, and they decided to say it backwards for luck."

I tried not to laugh. If I hadn't witnessed my brother, eyes closed, arms locked with his fellow bandmates, earnestly chanting mumbo jumbo, I wouldn't have believed it. But there it was, happening right in front of me.

The boys broke off with another cheer and gathered their instruments. Ray went down the line of musicians, slapping palms. When he came to me, he paused, then shook my hand awkwardly. His palm was sweaty and warm.

"You're on," he said. "Good luck!"

I made my way to the microphone at the centre of the stage. I know I must have walked there, but I can't recall the feel of the stage under my feet. People cheered before I said a single word. The sound was like a gust of wind, blowing away the what-ifs and filling my sails. I couldn't stop now if I wanted to — I was on a one way course and it was full-speed ahead. I wrapped my hand around the microphone stand, grateful for something solid to help ground me.

"Ladies and gentlemen, welcome to Sandy Shores!"

The cheering was so loud, I had to stop and wait for it to die down. I felt like a character from a book or a movie. Even the words I said felt like someone else's lines.

"My name is Maureen Starr, and I am pleased to welcome you to a night of music and dancing. First up, a locally grown band featuring some familiar faces."

I listed the names of the band members, who ran on stage to take their places as I called them. Again, the screaming was so loud I doubt anyone could hear me. It seemed pretty obvious that everyone knew who the boys were, though. They were so cool, nodding curtly at the audience and then looking away, tinkering with their instruments, as if they were completely oblivious to their screaming fans. But out of the corner of my eye I saw Bo fumble with a cord and I knew he was more nervous than he was letting on.

"And, finally, Paul Cracker!"

Cracker was the opposite of cool. He ran in like a cat let out of a bag, doing a whole lap of the stage before barrelling into me. He made a big show of looking embarrassed — took a deep bow, fixed the hem of my shorts and patted my ponytail to make sure I was all in one piece — then grabbed the microphone with two hands and apologized.

"I deeply, deeply apologize, Miss Starr. Will you ever forgive me?"

I pretended to think about it for a minute, which made Cracker fall to his knees, his hands clasped together, pleading. The audience laughed, and someone yelled, "Aw, come on! Give him a break!"

"You're forgiven," I said.

The audience cheered, then whistled as Cracker kissed me on the cheek. I fanned myself as if I were about to swoon and hurried off to the wings. I ran down the stairs and into the crowd as Bo's guitar roared to life. I was exhilarated. I'd heard Mimi, Bo and Gwen talk about the rush of performing, but until that moment I had never felt it for myself. I felt superhuman. Ray was standing against the wall, waiting for me. There must have been twenty people packed into that little corner, but all I could see was him. My superhuman sight locked onto him and drew me in.

"You were great!" he yelled, his mouth next to my ear.

I hoped the band would play forever, just so Ray would have to keep speaking to me like that. His breath against the nape of my neck made me shiver.

"Everybody loved you," he continued. "I knew they would."

Ray was grinning at me and I grinned back. I wondered which of us had the bigger smile.

As the boys eased into their set, I relaxed a little and started scanning the crowd. From my spot against the wall, I tried to get a glimpse of Mimi or Daddy, but I couldn't see past the first few rows of people. It was hard to believe that this room was the same place I had watched Gwen spin across, empty except for us and the dust motes.

The crowd was going crazy for Wide Mouth Bass. And it wasn't just the young people, everyone was smiling and nodding along. A few people were clapping and shaking their heads at each other, as if to say, Can you believe this? As fizzy and exhilarated as I felt, one thing niggled at my happiness like a toothache. Daddy wasn't here. I scanned the crowds again and again. In that sea of happy, impressed faces, his was the one I wanted to see the most. If only he could see what I had done, bringing these people together at Sandy Shores, pulling off a major event, surely he would feel confident leaving me in charge one day.

Eventually, the boys' set came to an end, and I wormed my way through the crush of people and ran back on stage to announce Gwen. "Our next performer is Gwen Cates, who some of you know as our dance teacher here at Sandy Shores."

Someone whistled and the crowd laughed.

"In addition to being a professionally trained ballerina, Gwen is a star in the making. Today she is going to sing a song for you written by Bo Starr, who is yet another — *star* — on the rise!"

A couple of people groaned at the joke, but more people laughed. I loved hosting. I got a thrill from making the audience laugh, even if it was at my bad jokes.

I turned to make my way off the stage and was struck still by the sight of Gwen, waiting for her entrance. She was wearing a dress I had never seen before, simple and white, with a round neckline and an overlay of lace, a narrow yellow belt buckled around her waist. She had tucked a sprig of blue flowers behind one ear. It was a bit like seeing a ghost, for here was the Gwendolyn I remembered from so many years ago, only more grown up. She looked like a fairy bride with her blond hair and pale dress. She didn't seem nervous at all. It reminded me of how she would dance on her own after class, as if she were completely alone, oblivious to my presence and comfortable in her own skin.

As I passed, she grabbed my fingers and squeezed lightly. Our eyes locked for one second. When she smiled, it looked a little sad. I wondered if maybe she was more nervous than she let on, or perhaps she was sad that her mother couldn't be here. I was about to ask what was wrong when she mouthed two words to me and turned away. It happened so quickly I couldn't tell what the words were, but I could ask her later.

Then she started to sing, and there wasn't a single person in the room who wasn't hanging on her every note. Her voice was so simple and beautiful, she didn't need backup dancers or a glittery dress or any smooth moves. She had ditched all of her girl-group shoulder rolls and finger wagging and stood at the microphone, one hand wrapped around the pole and the other hanging at her side. She didn't flirt with the audience; in fact, she barely looked at them. She sang out as if no one was there, with a slight nod to Bo as the song finished.

Silence, like a final note, hung in the air. It took a moment for people to shake themselves from Gwen's spell.

When they did, they burst into eager applause. Gwen smiled, nodded and then gestured to Bo, who did the same. As the applause rang on, they grinned at each other shyly, pleased but humbled by the response. Eventually the applause started to thin out, except for one person in the back. He was clapping madly, dog whistling and banging on the wall of the mess hall. A murmur spread through the crowd as people craned their necks and shifted, trying to get a glimpse of Gwen's fanatical admirer.

"Settle down there, buddy, and we'll do another," Bo said lightly into the microphone.

"I don't think so," the voice called out. "I've seen enough."

My entire body stiffened, and my heart fell all the way to the soles of my feet as Johnny Skins pushed his way through the crowd and hauled himself on stage. The murmuring grew into a dull roar as people started to recognize him. All of the colour drained from Gwen's cheeks as she backed away from the microphone. Bo looked puzzled, trying to figure out how he knew the man coming toward him.

Then a single voice rose above the crowd.

"It's him! It's Johnny Skins!"

Now the mess hall was full of screaming girls and the audience surged toward Johnny. Bo looked back at Gwen, who was hovering at the back of the stage like a deer in head-lights. Bo went to her, carefully taking her arm. There was so much tenderness in his reaction, that all the air was sucked right out of me and the truth exploded in front of my eyes like fireworks. Bo and Gwen. Why hadn't I seen it before?

I wasn't the only one who got it. Johnny took the abandoned microphone for himself.

"Well, hi there, Sandy Shores! It's swell to see you, too! Wasn't that nice? Wasn't that just the most goddamn nicest thing you've ever seen? Two kids in love, makin' a song."

"Please, let me though!" I cried, struggling uselessly against the hot bodies. Suddenly the mess hall felt too small, too crowded; it had become dangerous. My super-human strength was gone and I had to resort to ducking under sweaty arms and elbowing my way through the swarming mob.

"Come on back here and say hello, Dolly," Johnny sneered. "Oh, right, you're going by Gwen now. Is that what your boyfriend here calls you?"

Gwen started to shake. Bo led her toward the wings. Cracker appeared in the doorway, looking concerned. Johnny turned his attention back to the crowd and pouted. It was an ugly, cartoonish expression.

"Aw, we frightened poor Dolly away! There she goes, kids! Off into the woods with a different guy. He looks like the lead singer of your hometown band! Watch out, Bo, ladies love a leading man!"

Finally I reached the front of the crowd.

"Johnny, stop!" I screamed, slamming my open palms on the stage. It was no use. Even if he'd wanted to, he could never hear my voice over the excited crowd. I looked over my shoulder, searching for Daddy, Ray or somebody who could help, but all I could see were strangers, pressing in on me from all sides.

"Well, what can you expect from a dancer, right?" Johnny jeered.

Bo returned from the wings, having left both Gwen and his guitar with Cracker. He approached Johnny warily, hands out in front of him, showing he meant no harm. "Hey, cut it out, man." He had to yell to be heard. "We were just singing."

Johnny laughed. It wasn't a pleasant sound. "Cut it out, man?" Johnny laughed again. "Who do you think you are, a big shot? Hey, Sandy Shores, let me ask you a question. Who do you want to hear? Me—" Johnny pointed at himself and let the roaring of the crowd wash over him. Then he held his hand up for silence and hitched his thumb in Bo's direction, "—or this kid?"

People continued to scream, as if it were all part of the show.

"Looks like you've got a lot of fans out there, Mr. Big Shot. So why do you have to go after someone else's girl, huh? You think you can just help yourself and get away with it?"

Johnny was closing in on Bo, who continued to stand his ground. Bo was at least a head taller, but he wasn't nearly as angry as Johnny, who I knew was unpredictable and rash.

"Listen, you've got it all wrong," he said. "I was helping her out with a song, that's all."

He's lying, I thought. Johnny said that Gwen had stopped writing him letters. And the reason Ray recognized her shorts that night was because Gwen had been sneaking out to see Wide Mouth Bass play. Then she was so upset when I told her Johnny had called — not because she didn't want us to know about her secret rock star boyfriend — but because she didn't want Johnny to find out about Bo. They had been carrying on this whole time, and I hadn't noticed. How could I have been so stupid?

Johnny was laughing like a maniac, slapping his leg and whooping. The audience was beginning to get antsy. They were starting to clue in that something was wrong. Johnny jabbed Bo in the chest and leaned in. I could barely hear him over the rumble of the crowd.

"Right. A song. That's always how it starts, isn't it? I should know. Look, let's call it a day. We've both been had by the same girl. We're not the first two guys that's ever happened to, am I right?" Johnny spoke into the microphone and asked the crowd, "Who out there knows what it's like to be had by a cheating woman?"

No one seemed to know how to respond. A few people laughed and someone cheered weakly. Then Johnny extended his hand to Bo, who looked at it but didn't move to shake it. In that split-second pause, Johnny drew back and thrust his arm forward in a punch. I heard the crack as his knuckles connected with Bo's jaw, and I felt as if someone had punched me in the stomach. Bo spun around with the impact and landed on the stage with a thud.

There was a collective intake of breath, and then the screaming began again — but this time it was shrill and panicked. I scrambled to pull myself up on the stage, but someone grabbed me around my waist and yanked me away.

"Let me go!" I screamed. "Bo!"

It was Ray, his mouth by my ear again. "No, Reenie! You'll get hurt!"

Bo had rolled onto all fours, his hair hanging in his eyes. Two members of his band, including Cracker, had appeared on stage and stood between Bo and Johnny, yelling threats. Two men I didn't recognize jumped on stage to give them a hand. On the floor, the crowd was split into bloodthirsty spectators, chanting "fight, fight, fight," girls crying and wild-eyed women and children who couldn't get out of there fast enough. I leapt at the stage again, and Ray picked me up and carried me through the crowd. I twisted in his arms, demanding to be let down.

• Over Ray's shoulder, I watched as Johnny slugged another

man who had been trying to pin him to the stage.

"Bo!" I cried. "What about Bo?"

"He'll be fine; there are lots of guys in there on his side. It's not safe in there right now."

I screamed for my dad, tears streaming down my face. When we finally made our way out of the mess hall, Ray set me down gently on a log.

"My dad," I said. "You have to find my dad."

He knelt in front of me, hands on both shoulders, and looked me right in the eyes. "I'm going to find him," he said. "But promise me you won't go back in there."

I nodded and Ray squeezed my hand one final time before sprinting off toward the lawn we were using as the parking lot. I closed my eyes and took a long, deep breath through my nose, trying to ignore the shouting. I tried to calm down by focussing on the damp smell and rough grooves of the log beneath me. When I opened my eyes, I felt clearer and more determined. I couldn't sit around and wait for things to happen. I had to find Daddy myself.

The Getaway

Even away from the crush of people stumbling out of the mess hall, Sandy Shores was buzzing with excitement. I couldn't find Daddy or Ray in the parking area, so I started looking everywhere else I could think of. Daddy was nowhere to be found.

I asked after him with each person I met, but no one had seen him. There were people everywhere. Guests had gathered around the firepit and were trading their versions of events. On the front lawn, in between the tightly packed cars, kids were huddled, gossiping. Some of them had gone down to the beach and were goofing off in the sand. As I ran through the resort, I caught snatches of conversations.

"I can't believe that was really Johnny Skins. Wait till I tell my sister."

"Did you see Bo hit the ground? I thought he was out for sure."

"And then my husband climbed up to give that poor boy a hand. I told him not to, because of his heart, but he just went ahead and got in there."

"It's that music they listen to — it makes them go crazy."

I listened for any mention of Daddy, but no one had seen or heard from him. All that gossip passed me by, like someone was turning a dial on a radio.

I met Bert rushing out the back door of the lodge. His shirt was untucked, and he had a daub of shaving cream on his neck. Two of Johnny's band members were lounging on the steps, smoking.

"What's going on?" Bert asked.

"Johnny's out of control. He attacked my brother," I shouted.

Bert looked suspicious, but not all that surprised. "What did your brother do to him?"

"He didn't *do* anything!" I yelled. "Johnny is crazy!"

Bert held his hands up in surrender and tried to calm me down in a voice that only managed to irk me even more. "I'm sure we can work things out, why don't we just get the boys in a room together . . ."

"It's a little late for that," one of the boys muttered. "The kid's long gone."

"What are you saying, Don?" Bert asked. "Did you see something?"

Don took a long drag on his cigarette before replying, "I saw the blond kid book it to the road. He had a couple of bags with him."

"How do you know it was Bo?" I demanded.

"The kid I saw was hurt. He was holding his jaw like maybe it was broken or something."

I pushed Don aside and tore up the stairs and into Gwen's room without knocking. Gwen was nowhere to be found. Her bed was unmade, but otherwise there were no signs that anyone had been staying there. The assorted bottles of shampoos and creams had been cleared from the wardrobe. There were no clothes to be seen on the floor or in the closet, and every last letter was gone. It looked like she had been planning to leave.

I thought about the last time I had seen Gwen, when she had squeezed my fingers before taking to the stage. She had said something, but I couldn't hear it over the noise in the mess hall. Now I wondered if it had been goodbye.

I ran down the stairs and into the dining hall, expecting to find no one. The four big windows along the front of the room, looking out over the lake, framed the landscape into neat squares, like four perfectly hung paintings — the kind people would pay a lot of money for. A woman was silhouetted in the furthest window, one hand resting on the table, the other in her lap. She was looking out over the dark lake. It was Mimi.

I called her name but she didn't stir. I hadn't seen her at all after the catastrophe. I had assumed she had run for Daddy, but then why was she sitting here, alone?

"Mimi? It's me, Reenie."

I approached with caution, like you approach a strange dog. I couldn't tell what kind of mood she was in, but I knew it wasn't one of her better ones. As I got closer I saw that Mimi had her scarf full of treasures open on her lap, the old locket wound between her fingers. She was gripping the chain so tight her knuckles were bone-white in the darkness.

"Mimi, have you seen Gwen?"

She shook her head, but didn't turn to look at me.

"She's missing." I added, "Bo is, too."

"All this time I was worried about you." The sound of her voice was like a cold finger drawing the length of my spine.

"Worried about what?" I asked.

"Gwen. I thought she might be a bad influence on you. I never once thought about him."

I inched closer, despite all the impulses in my body that were telling me I didn't want to be here. Mimi's voice was so odd, and I wished she would just turn and look at me. If I could just see her face, I could tell what kind of mood she was in.

Mimi had opened the locket, and the curl of almost-white hair lay on the table beside her. Irritation prickled at my skin like heat rash. Now was not the time to be stuck in the past, getting romantic about old baby things.

"Did you hear me, Mimi? They're missing. Bo was hurt. We have to find them. This isn't the time to be playing with Scarlett's baby hair."

Mimi looked at me then, and the sadness in her eyes was so deep, I thought I might drown.

"Oh, Reenie, it's not Scarlett's hair. It's Gwen's."

Mimi's secret

I was aware of other noises, gravel crunching under tires as car after car pulled away from our front lawn, laughter drifting up from the beach, but these sounds felt far away, as if they belonged to another world. In the world of the lodge, Mimi and I were the only living souls. When Mimi started to talk her voice was so low I had to lean in to hear her, but I was afraid of getting too close; her words were too alarming. Each one set off an explosion in my brain and blew apart the entire landscape of everything I had known to be true.

"When I first moved to Toronto, I felt like I had won the lottery. I had new, exciting friends, men were sending me flowers, taking me to dinner . . . It was intoxicating, all that attention, all that freedom. It was wartime and everybody was living like there was no tomorrow, and why not? The papers made it sound like there wasn't going to be one. I was reckless. We all were."

I took two steps backward, needing to get away from her words. I felt I would be safer at a distance. My movement must have caught her eye, because she turned to look at me with beseeching eyes.

"Believe me, Reenie, this is not the kind of picture a mother wants to paint for her children, but you need to know the truth now. When I realized I was pregnant, I panicked. I couldn't look after a baby. I was so ashamed. No one could know. Not the father, not my family, no one. The only people who knew were Grace and her husband. They took pity on me and let me stay at their family's summer place when I started to show. It was surprisingly easy to keep it a secret. I was terrible at keeping in touch, so no one so much as batted an eye when I dropped off the map for six months."

As Mimi's story poured out, I had to keep reminding myself that this was a true story, not the plot of a play she had been in once.

"I knew I couldn't keep the baby. That was never part of the plan. But the thought of giving it away to a stranger was . . ." Mimi paused, flexing her hands as if they had fallen asleep. The chain fell from her fingers and landed in the scarf in a pool of burnished metal links. "Well, it was harder than I'd expected. Grace had been having some trouble conceiving and it just seemed like fate. A little cruel and twisted, but fate all the same. And so the arrangements were made. Grace agreed to keep me informed on the progress of our little girl — that's how I thought of her, as mine and Grace's — but we agreed that Gwendolyn was never to know." Mom paused to wipe her eyes, which were starting to fill up. Even in her sadness, it was an elegant gesture. "To this day, she doesn't know she was adopted.

"Afterward, I tried to carry on as if nothing had changed. I moved back to my old rooming house, went to auditions, but it wasn't the same. Then I met your father. He was so sweet and funny and full of plans . . . So when he asked me to marry him and live up north, I said yes. We hadn't known each other long, but it just felt right. And here was a chance to leave the past in Toronto and start fresh.

"Bo was born the year after we were married. I'd wanted to start over, with a family of my own. Grace wrote and kept me informed on how Gwendolyn was doing. When she told me that Gwen was going to ballet school, it made me so proud. I didn't make it as an actress, but maybe my daughter would find success on the stage.

"But a few months ago, Grace told me Gwen was in trouble. She was sneaking out at night and came in reeking of alcohol. She'd been skipping classes and was threatening to leave ballet altogether. I didn't want her to make the same mistakes I made. I thought I could help her. I thought if I could bring her here, I could keep her away from all those bad influences. I could keep an eye on her. Maybe we could even get to know each other . . ." Mimi sighed. "It was a selfish plan. I just wanted to know my little girl."

Somehow I found my voice. "But you had us," I said.

Mimi turned to look at me, and she smiled. It was a real smile, although it did little to calm the churning feeling in my stomach. "Yes. And I am so, so lucky to have you and Bo and Scarlett. You are the best children in the world. I want you to know that whenever I was sad, whenever I was . . . distant, it wasn't because of you or your brother or sister. It was never because of you."

"Last summer, when you disappeared, you went to visit her," I said. It hurt to say those words out loud, like each one was a shard of glass I had to swallow.

"Not at first," Mimi said. "At first my head was such a mess I didn't know what I was doing. I just needed to get away. I caught a bus headed for the city, and eventually I made my way to Grace's." Tears glistened on Mimi's cheeks. "She wasn't even there. I felt like such a fool. I had frightened everyone so badly, and Gwendolyn wasn't even there . . ."

"Does Daddy know?" I asked.

She nodded. "Your father is the best man I know," she said simply.

I looked out at the horizon, wondering how to go forward from this moment. I had watched the sun sink into the lake more times than I could recall. It was something I took for granted. The sun set and it would rise again tomorrow. But tomorrow the world it revealed would be completely different from the world I had grown up in. In this new world, Gwen was my sister, something I had wished for secretly time and time again. Now that wish had come true. It made me uneasy. I know it's silly to think a person has the power to wish something true, but part of me wondered.

I wished I could take it back.

A car sped into the driveway, two yellow beams moving like ghosts across Mimi's stone face. The shrill sound of squealing rubber made me flinch, but Mimi remained motionless, even as the doors slammed and the sound of Bo yelling grew louder as he and Daddy neared the lodge. Gwen walked a few steps behind them, head down, like she was on her way to a funeral. She was still wearing her white dress, which shone eerily in the moonlight.

My heart ached for Gwen. She seemed like a thwarted princess, now more than ever. She didn't even know she was adopted, let alone related to the boy she was in love with. My chest tightened. I needed to get out of there. I didn't want to be anywhere near Bo or Gwen when Mimi told them the truth. But I wasn't fast enough. I had barely made it halfway across the dining hall when the door swung open and Bo burst in, Daddy close behind him. Gwen hovered in the door, looking unsure of herself.

"I found them halfway to Orillia, speeding down the back roads," Daddy said to no one in particular. "I was watching over the cars and saw them leave. That boy with the eyebrows was driving them, the singer."

"His name is Paul," Bo said curtly, "and he wasn't speeding, and we weren't breaking any laws! Stop treating us like criminals!"

He grabbed Gwen's hand and pulled her closer to Mimi. For a moment I thought he was going to get on his knees to implore her. He must have thought better of it, because instead he smoothed his hair and lowered his voice.

"I'm going to Toronto with Gwen. I want to be a musician. There's nothing here for me anymore."

"Of course there is," Mimi said, looking hurt.

"You can't stop us," Bo said in a valiant attempt at controlling his nerves.

Mimi stood then, regaining her composure. Her chin was set at the exact same angle as Bo's. They were both stubborn, but there was more steel in Mimi's gaze.

"I can, and I will," she said. She sounded calm and confident, like she was ready to win this argument. I couldn't remember a time when she seemed as formidable. Even when she decided to bring Gwen up north as the dance teacher, she was eager for Daddy to agree. The Mimi standing here now, staring down her most stubborn child, wasn't looking for anyone's approval. Bo must have thought so, too, because I saw a moment's hesitation in his eyes.

"I don't get you," he said, throwing up his hands. "I would have thought *you* of all people would understand. All you ever wanted was to get out of this place. You did once, remember? Or did you forget the time you just abandoned your family?"

"I remember," Mimi said sadly.

"I'm not staying here. You can't make me. If I don't leave now, then some other time, and soon! And Gwen's coming with me."

"You're right, Bo. I can't make you stay. Not forever. But your future is not with Gwen, not the way you think. There is something you need to know," Mimi said calmly. "Both of you."

"Reenie."

The tone in Daddy's voice told me it was time to go. I didn't need to be told twice.

I ran through the lodge, across the dark lawn and crashed into the woods. I ran faster and harder than I ever had before. Branches whipped at my face and scratched my arms, but nothing could slow me down. My toe caught on something and my ankle twisted, but I ignored the pinch and kept on going. I skidded to a stop by a birch tree — tall and white as a sentinel — pausing to lean forward with my hands on my thighs until my breath came evenly again and I could think rationally.

It was darker now; night had finally descended, but I knew this place tree by tree, stone by stone. Carefully, I picked my way back, toeing my way through exposed roots and rocks and slippery patches of crabgrass, until I emerged from the woods behind Monarch Cottage.

Years ago I'd convinced Daddy to give the cottages names instead of numbers. I made a list and we voted on them as a family. Some of my favourites, like Silver Shingles and The Sand Castle were voted down. "Too girly," Bo protested. Instead, we agreed on simple names, like Pebble Cottage and Birch Cottage. Bo and I made signs for each one, using Daddy's wood burner to write the name on a plank of wood. Bo did the burning and I varnished them when they were done. Every time I walk by and see the signs hanging on the cottages, pride flutters in my chest.

Behind Monarch Cottage, a patch of milkweed grows as tall as my waist, with leaves as big as Scarlett's hand. In early summer, caterpillars striped yellow, white and black gorge themselves on the milky leaves until they grow fat like sausages. Then one day they hang upside down and start spinning themselves cocoons as green as celery. It takes a week for them to build them. Every year I plonk myself in the grass nearby and watch them. It's almost like being hypnotized. The walls of the cocoons become translucent, until one day you're staring at the fully formed orange and black wing of a Monarch butterfly.

On hatching days, I used to pack a peanut butter sandwich and a Thermos of Mimi's sun tea and find a spot in the tall grass, my back against the sun-baked boards of Monarch Cottage. It was one of my favourite places in the whole world. At least it used to be. In the distance I could always hear the sound of kids shrieking and laughing as they splashed in the water, but all their noise was almost lost under the hum of the bees and cicadas that surrounded me. I'd watch as the brand new butterflies emerged, wet and glistening. It would take at least an hour before their wings were dry and they were able to fly.

Only I hadn't come this year. I had been too busy, first with Gwen, and then plotting Johnny's visit. It hadn't even crossed my mind until now. Fresh tears spilled down my cheeks. I had missed my chance. I had missed that magical moment when the butterflies threw themselves into the breeze, dipping woozily in the air before fluttering away to begin their new lives. I could use that magic now, something beautiful and miraculous to wonder at, instead of all the secrets and confusion that were waiting for me beyond the sanctuary of Monarch Cottage. Too much was changing too fast.

I wished I could turn back the summers to when I was nine, eight, even seven — and hold on to them as long as possible, because they were perfect. If only I had known it then. I would trade everything — Gwen, Ray, the truth — to go back again. No one had ever told me that growing up would hurt like this.

I sniffed, drawing my arm across my face, mopping up the tears and snot that had collected there. I couldn't stay here forever. No amount of wishing would change anything. Eventually, I'd have to go home, look Mimi in the eye, see Gwen and Bo and continue on.

It was almost funny, if you think about it. All summer long, all I'd wanted was for people to treat me like an adult, and now that they were, all I wanted was to be eight years old again, waiting for the butterflies to hatch.

*　*　*

I managed to make my way home and crawl into bed without running into a single person. I didn't think I could bear more tears, mine or anyone else's. But later in the night I awoke to cold little feet kneading my leg. I rolled over to discover a stowaway in my bed.

"Scarlett," I hissed. "Stop kicking me."

Scarlett moaned in her sleep and tossed violently, waking herself up in the process.

"Are you awake, Reenie?"

"I am now," I muttered.

Scarlett sighed and snuggled into me, fitting her head between my cheek and my shoulder. "Your shoulder is bony," she complained.

"Then use your pillow like a normal person," I said.

Scarlett continued to wiggle around the bed, trying to get comfortable. After a while, she asked, "What's going to happen?"

"With what?"

"Gwen."

"So you heard?"

"I was listening outside the door," Scarlett admitted. "Is she really our sister?"

"Yes, she's our half-sister."

"We look alike," Scarlett mused.

"You do," I agreed. I'd noticed a few times how similar Gwen and Scarlett or Gwen and Mimi looked. Now that I knew the resemblance was more than just a coincidence, it seemed as obvious as blackflies in June.

"Will she stay here now?" Scarlett asked.

"Probably not. She has a family in Toronto. Plus she wants to be a singer."

"She sounded nice tonight, even better than at campfire."

"I thought so, too."

"Will we go visit her?"

"Maybe."

"Do you want a big sister?"

"I don't know. Do you?"

"I've already got one."

"I meant another one."

"I don't really need two sisters," Scarlett said. "But I don't want to hurt her feelings. I like Gwen."

"I like her, too."

"But not as much as I like you."

"You better not," I said, tickling her. Scarlett giggled and the sound was so normal it almost brought tears to my eyes.

"Now there are six Starrs," Scarlett mused.

"Gwen isn't really a Starr," I said. "She isn't Daddy's daughter."

"Can't we adopt her?"

"I think she's too old. Plus, maybe she doesn't want to be adopted. She has her own father and mother. This is all new to her, too."

"I'd rather be a Starr than a Cates," Scarlett decided. "I'd rather be a Starr than anyone else."

"Me, too," I said.

Fishing

I was up early, roused from my sleep by the lonely call of a mourning dove. It sounded extra sad, as if it had looked inside my head and was cooing in sympathy. I wondered where its mate was, and why she didn't respond. I scooted to the edge of the bed, careful not to wake Scarlett, and peered out the window, searching for the bird. The morning was still grey, wrapped in swaths of cottony mists the sun had yet to burn through. Eventually I spotted it as it took off: a plump grey shape against the colourless sky, perhaps in search of a duet partner. As I watched it fly toward the beach, I spied Daddy leave the lodge and head down to the dock.

Suddenly it felt like the most important thing in the world to get there before he left. The thought of Daddy pulling away from the dock, without me aboard, filled me with red-hot panic. I flew out of bed, still wearing my clothes from last night, and tore after him. I ran all the way there, shoeless, my heart throbbing in my throat. I had to get on the boat.

"Wait!" I cried, my bare feet slapping against the dock. "Wait! I want to come with you!"

When I finally got there, my breathing ragged and face

flushed, Daddy was looking up at me, concerned but also a little amused.

"Well, all right. I hear you. You better calm down or you'll scare the fish."

Daddy steadied the boat as I climbed in and made a spot for myself between a stained orange life vest and Daddy's big green tackle box. "Are you all right?" he asked, eyeing me carefully.

I nodded, yes, but didn't say a word. I didn't trust myself to speak. I turned my face away, looking out into the gauzy morning, as Daddy started the motor. The engine came to life with a wheeze and eventually settled into a regular putt-putt rhythm as we sliced through the lake, leaving Sandy Shores behind us. I watched the dock and the lodge grow smaller and smaller, until they dissolved into the misty morning like sugar in water.

A lesser fisherman would be lost in all that morning mist, but Daddy knew the lake like the words to his favourite song, and I trusted his sense of direction as he steered us into the unknown — one hand on the engine and the other holding his tattered old fishing hat on his head. We weren't going full-speed, but the sputtering of the engine was too loud to talk over anyway. As we neared his favourite fishing spot, he cut the engine. "Can't let the fish know we're coming," he explained.

We drifted for a while, through lily pads as big as dinner plates. I let my hand trail over the side of the boat, my fingers pulling up tangles of roots, like handfuls of long green spaghetti.

I hadn't been fishing with Daddy in ages. We used to go all the time. We'd leave so early that sometimes we were back before anyone had had breakfast. I looked down and saw that my old rod was still in the bottom of the boat. It was slim, painted forest green like the tackle box. I picked it up and tested the line's tension. I was surprised at how light it felt in my hand.

"Worm or lure?" Daddy asked.

"Lure," I said, and he opened his tackle box to let me choose.

The tackle box expanded into three compartments, each one packed with oddly shaped and coloured fishing lures. Seeing them was like discovering a box of forgotten child-hood toys. Their names came rushing back to me — spin-nerbait, spooks, jitterbug, bucktail, crankbait — some were made of wood and jointed in the middle, like insects. They were painted to look like real fish, with yellow eyes and white bellies. Others looked more like birds, or strange fish-bird hybrids, brightly painted, with whirly bits and feathered tails that stirred the water in patterns that attracted hungry fish.

I almost always chose the same lure. It was a plastic mermaid with a black tail and black hair. She had a triple hook at the end of her tail and in her navel. Daddy said it was more of a novelty lure than anything else, something he had picked up as a souvenir, but she was my favourite. Daddy used to call her the Lady of the Lures. He kidded that if I ever turned into a fish, the Lady of the Lures is how he would catch me. I knew he was teasing, but there was a time when I was young enough to wonder if such a transformation was actually possible.

I dug through the lures until I found her. There were chips in her paint and she wasn't as grand as I remembered her, but she was there all the same, waiting for me. I felt a twinge of guilt, as if she had been aware of my absence and felt abandoned.

"I should have known," Daddy said, as I secured her to the end of my line.

I waited for him to say more, but the silence stretched out as long as winter, and I eventually turned back to my own line.

"Tell me about the time you broke your rod," I said. I had heard the story so many times I could tell it myself, but I needed to hear him tell it again.

"First of all, it wasn't me who broke the rod, it was Big Sandy," Daddy said, settling into the story. Big Sandy is a legendary muskie that lives in the lake. Fishermen have been trying to catch her for years, but she always gets away. "And it was a damn good rod, too. It belonged to my father who passed it on to me when I was sixteen."

"Bo's age," I realized. When I was younger and listening to this story, sixteen seemed so old. It was practically grown up. Now that Bo was sixteen, and I was only a few years away from it myself, it seemed frighteningly young. It gave the story a whole different colour.

Daddy nodded. "That's right. I thought I was a big shot fisherman back then. I'd caught more than my fair share of some good-sized pike, which you know about."

I nodded. Everyone knew about Daddy's fishing prowess. There was a newspaper cutting from an angling contest he had won, when he was only fourteen, framed and hanging in the office. In the picture, he was squinting in the sun, holding the award-winning fish with both hands.

"Well, like many fishermen before me, I thought I would go after Big Sandy. The last anyone had seen of her was the fall of '37. A guest by the name of Henry Tate had her at the end of his line but she got away, taking his best lure with her. He said she was at least six feet long. Later that same day his boat was overturned. Some people said he hit a submerged log, but he swore that Big Sandy swam right under the boat and tipped it over. He thought she did it on purpose."

This part of the story made me shiver. When I pictured Big Sandy, I imagined a wingless, legless dragon, with a pointed snout full of teeth and muddy scales as tough as nails.

"Now, whether or not that's true, no one will ever know. The point is, she's a dangerous fish, and damn hard to catch. So the next year, I get it in my head that my knack for fishing along with my father's rod is a deadly combination. Deadly for Big Sandy that is, not for me."

Daddy paused and cast off. The line was so transparent, and the morning had grown so bright, that I couldn't see it arc against the sky. But I heard the zinging noise it made as it sliced through the air, the lure eventually landing with a plonk.

"I spent most of my sixteenth summer in this very spot, waiting for Big Sandy. Most people thought I was crazy, or at the very least, a lazy son of a gun who was doing his darndest to get out of his chores." Daddy winked. "I was a man obsessed. I stopped fishing for anything else, throwing everything I caught back in disgust. It had to be Big Sandy or nothing at all.

"And then one day, I got a bite. It was early, about this time, in the dead of summer. The woods were already steaming, and it was so still you could hear a door slam clear across the lake. I knew it was her right away. The pull was unlike anything I had ever had on my line before, like a sea monster had clamped down on my lure and was going to pull me all the way out to the ocean. I stood, trying to get leverage as the rod started to slip from my grasp. I was gripping the reel so hard I could feel blisters forming, but

I was not going to give up without a fight. Then the rod snapped, and I fell forward, hitting my chin against the edge of the boat. I bit my tongue and tasted blood and sure enough, when I caught my reflection in the lake, I looked like something out of one of those horror movies you kids like so much — blood gushing down my chin.

"I took off my shirt and dipped it in the water so I could swab the blood from my face before heading for home. I was leaning over the side of the boat, trying to use my reflection as a guide, when this enormous fish came lunging up toward me. I reared back into the boat just as it surfaced. It snapped its jaws and I saw my lure, lodged in its mouth, before it disappeared back under the water."

I peered over the edge of the boat at the murky, greenish water, imagining the head of an enormous fish coming toward me.

"I figured she could smell the blood from my cut. That damn fish thought she could make a meal out of your old dad, but it was not to be. Though I wasn't completely unscathed; she left me with half a fishing rod and a nice little memento to remember her by."

Daddy pointed to his face. A small scar, about the length of my thumbnail and the width of a pencil, split his chin in two. When I was little and he would tell this story, I would trace the puckered silvery skin with my pinkie and marvel at how he had narrowly escaped being eaten by a large, man-eating fish. I knew now that muskie don't eat people, but at the time it scared me enough that I kept my fingers and toes inside the boat whenever we drifted into the weedy shallows that Daddy called Muskie Country.

"I haven't told that story in a long time," Daddy said. "I thought maybe you'd grown out of it."

"Never," I said. "I love that story."

"It doesn't seem to have the same effect on your sister."

I smiled. Scarlett hated fishing more than anything in the world. She claimed the smell of the boat made her "seasick" to her stomach.

"It doesn't scare you like it used to," Daddy pointed out. He smiled sadly. "You've grown too big and too smart to be fooled by my tall tales."

Tears burned my eyes. "I don't feel grown up," I mumbled, partly to myself and partly so Daddy could hear. "Everything I do goes wrong."

"You mean the party," he said softly.

"Are you mad at me, Daddy?" I asked, my voice barely above a whisper. I was so ashamed, I kept my eyes on the murky water, afraid of seeing the disappointment in Daddy's eyes.

"Reenie, I'm not pleased with your decision to go ahead and hire that rat Johnny what's-his-name to come up here without consulting me or your mother first. That sort of decision requires a background check and a few phone calls to make sure we know who we're getting and what to expect." He paused, and I waited for him to reel in his line, check his lure and cast again off before he resumed speaking. "But I know your heart was in the right place, and I'm pretty confident you won't pull something like that again."

"I won't, Daddy. I swear."

"Plus, you aren't responsible for that hoodlum's actions."

A little part of me felt relieved, but no matter what Daddy said, I couldn't shake the heavy feeling that I *was* responsible.

"But if I hadn't invited him, none of this would have happened," I protested, bitterly. "I thought I was so smart, throwing one big party to make everyone happy. I wanted to surprise Gwen and give Bo a chance to play for a real audience. I thought all the excitement would make Mimi happy, and most of all, I wanted you to see that I have what it takes to run Sandy Shores some day." I paused to take a shaky breath. "But all I did was mess everything up."

Daddy shook his head. "No, Reenie. If anything, what you did brought everything out into the open. We were headed for disaster the minute Gwen walked in the door. I had a feeling it wasn't going to be the cozy reunion your mother was hoping for, but it was something she needed to do. Keeping that secret all these years has been hard on her."

I tried to imagine what it must have been like for Mimi, having a secret child that she could never talk about. When people asked her how many children she had, did she immediately think four, and then have to check herself before responding three? When she sent a birthday card every year for Gwen, did she think about telling her the truth? The only place Mimi could be Gwen's mother was inside her head. Maybe that's where her moods came from; when her secret threatened to spill out into the world, she had to lock herself up and be alone with it for a while.

"Is that why she gets so sad?" I asked.

Daddy thought before answering.

"That's part of it. Some people can't help feeling sad. Her mother was the same way."

"Really?"

I had no memories of my grandmother, who died when I was four. The only image I had of her came from a photograph Mimi kept in her family album. In it, she is sitting with baby Bo on her lap. She is square and stout and looks nothing like Mimi. It's hard to tell anything about what she was like because she still has that stiff expression that people wore in old photos. I knew that she and Mimi didn't get along, and that she thought acting was frivolous. Mimi had gone to the city against her wishes. If Daddy was right, then it seems like the only thing they shared was sadness.

"That sort of sadness runs in families sometimes," Daddy said.

"I don't want to be like that."

"You aren't."

"How do you know?"

Daddy smiled. "Reenie Starr, you are one hundred percent your father's daughter. You may have your mother's eyes and her charms, but you and I fell from the same tree."

"What about Bo?"

Daddy looked at his line, sighed, then continued, "The fact is, your brother has been gunning to get out of here for ages, even before Gwen showed up. I didn't want to think about it too much, but you can't look the other way forever."

"You saw all those people, Daddy. They were all here to see Bo! Maybe he can make it as a musician. Besides, you've got me. I'll stay here and run things, Daddy. I never want to leave. I know I made a big mistake, but I'm learning. If you teach me everything you know, I swear, when I'm older, I can run it. Nobody loves Sandy Shores more than I do."

"I know that, Maureen. I've always known that. Probably longer than you." Daddy took off his big floppy hat that smelled like the boathouse and dropped it over my head. It was too big for me, and fell over my eyes. I laughed and pushed it back. Daddy was looking right at me. "Does this mean you aren't going to run away and join the circus? Be a big-time ballerina?"

I groaned. "Ballerinas don't join the circus, Daddy. You

know that. Besides, as it turns out, I'm not very good at dancing."

"Don't sell yourself short. You're good at lots of things."

I huffed. I couldn't think of a single thing. "Oh really? Like what?" I asked.

"Like making people laugh, and taking care of Scarlett, and thinking of other people's feelings. You have a big heart, Reenie. That is something to be proud of."

The lure neared the boat, slurping and whirring through the water. I watched as Daddy reeled it in one last time, the blades dripping and glinting in the sun, which was now a blazing white disc in the sky. We were in for a hot day.

"That's enough for today," Daddy said, smiling sadly. "Can't stay away forever."

As he set the lures back in the tackle box and prepared to head back to Sandy Shores, I thought about what he'd said. Maybe people would never ask me to sing for them, or whisper about what a beautiful dancer I was, but they laughed at my jokes. Guests were always happy to see me, and no matter what mood they were in when I stopped to talk to them, they were always smiling when I left. When Scarlett needed comfort, like last night, it was me she came to now. These *were* things to be proud of.

Daddy started the motor and the boat took off, whipping the still air into a breeze that tossed my hair about and reminded me how much I liked being on the water. I felt lighter than I had in days, maybe all summer long. So what if everything was upside down and inside out? I was still Reenie Starr of Sandy Shores. No one could take that away from me.

"I'm not going to run away," I shouted over the roar of the motor. "I could never leave this place."

I wasn't sure if Daddy could hear me, but I forgot that we were the same, and our ears knew how to adjust to the sounds of Sandy Shores, old motorboats included. He smiled and called back, "What did I tell you? You are your father's daughter."

* * *

After the spectacle of last night, Saturday at Sandy Shores felt deserted. Even checkout was subdued. Daddy and I manned the office together. He apologized profusely for the events of the night before, offering early bird rates to the guests as they left, but no one took him up on the offer. They thought he was overreacting. One customer said it was the most excitement he'd had all summer. "Just wait till I tell people I got the chance to take a swing at Johnny Skins," he boasted.

His wife beamed, slipping her arm through her husband's.

"I can't imagine what that poor boy would have done without you there," she said.

A record three couples and four families signed up for next summer at checkout. In a weird way, Johnny had done exactly what I hoped he would do; he'd put us on the map. People were talking about Sandy Shores.

A reporter came sniffing around, but Daddy remained tight-lipped, refusing to give a comment. He had struck a deal with Bert and both parties agreed never to speak of the Sandy Shores concert again. With time it would become a great legend. For years to come, people would call and ask to stay in the room that Johnny Skins had been in. Some places have ghosts or sea monsters, but at Sandy Shores we had Johnny Skins.

Sisters

Grace Cates arrived later that afternoon. She looked pale and drawn and wasn't as imposing as I remembered. She set up in my parents' bedroom, Daddy graciously moving into a spare guest room to give her and Mimi privacy. For the next few days she followed my mother like a shadow. They never seemed to be more than an arm's length away from each other, whispering or crying. I even saw them laughing a few times, despite everything that had gone on. Daddy asked Scarlett if she would like to spend the weekend at her friend Mary-Beth's house, but she refused, never straying far from the lodge and spending her nights in my bed.

Both Gwen and Bo shut themselves away from the world: Bo in his attic kingdom, Gwen locked in her room across the hall from mine. I found myself loitering outside her door five or six times that day, wondering if I should knock, like I had done earlier in the summer. I tried to imagine what Gwen was feeling but it was too hard to do. It was the kind of thing that just didn't happen in real life.

I knew that eventually she would be hungry, and I guessed that she would sneak down to the kitchen in the middle of the night. Sunday, after everyone had gone to bed, I slipped back down to the kitchen and sat on the floor, my back against the refrigerator, to wait for her. I read by flashlight until my eyes were so grainy I couldn't stand it. The first night I fell asleep and woke up as the sky was turning pink, and with just enough time to dash upstairs and sneak into bed before Elsa arrived. On the next night, I heard the stairs creak and I knew my plan had worked.

When Gwen came in, I had already closed my book and was smiling up at her, as if we had made plans to meet in the kitchen in the middle of the night. She took in the scene and scoffed, "That's a weird place to read."

"I was waiting for you."

"Can you move over? I need to get into the fridge. I'm starving."

I shimmied over and Gwen opened the refrigerator, found some leftover potato salad and plopped down on the floor beside me with a sigh.

"Go ahead. Say it," she said between spoonfuls of cold potatoes.

"Say what?"

"Say what everyone is thinking, 'Gee, Gwen, how can one person be such a complete and utter disaster?'"

Gwen's voice dripped with sarcasm. The acid in her voice made me flinch.

"I don't think you're a disaster," I protested.

"Really?" Gwen adopted a phony newscaster voice and continued, "Promising ballerina drops out of big-time ballet school, falls in with the wrong crowd, gets sent away to the country for safekeeping, where she promptly makes plans to run away with her own long-lost brother and causes a riot!" She dropped the voice and stabbed a slimy chunk of potato with such force that mayonnaise splattered along my arm.

"I think that pretty much defines disaster," she said.

"You didn't know he was your brother," I pointed out.

Gwen's head fell forward and she started to cry. It happened so quickly, I was caught off guard. It was alarming to see her without any bravado, like a turtle without its shell. She seemed so much younger, sniffling into her hands, shoulders shaking. I wiggled a little closer, trying to fit my arm around her shoulders, but she was too close to the refrigerator door.

"I'm sorry," she said between sobs. "I can't stop crying. Everything is so messed up."

"Do you want to get out of here?" I asked.

Gwen hiccupped. "What, now? Where would we go?"

"The beach. The water will clear your head."

I stood up, offering Gwen my hand. She blinked at it, as if she couldn't quite understand what it was doing in front of her. I wondered if I was being too bold, and whether it would have been better to sit tight and let her cry, But we needed to get out of that hot, stuffy kitchen. Gwen hadn't been out of the lodge in three whole days.

"Okay."

Gwen took my hand, and together we left the dark kitchen, full of brooding shadows and stale air, and escaped into the cool, clear night. It was so much brighter outside, with space to move and room to breathe. I let go of Gwen's clammy hand, stepped out of my slippers and ran through the grass, across the road and, finally, into the warm sands of the beach, stopping at the edge of the lake. My heels sunk into the wet sand and the water curled around my toes, coaxing me to go deeper. Within seconds, Gwen was beside me, breathing hard.

"It *is* a nice night," she said.

"Think you can beat me to the raft?" I asked.

Gwen started to speak, but I didn't wait around to hear her answer. I threw aside my big ratty nightshirt and ran straight into the lake. I gasped as the water made contact with my most sensitive places — between my legs and into my belly button and finally beneath my armpits — before I dove in and swam as hard as I could. I relished the drag of the water pulling at my face and hair, and wondered, not for the first time, if this was how fish felt. It was another world under the water, as strange as a different planet or a fairyland, where colours and shapes dissolved and the noise from above the surface was muffled beyond recognition. Underwater, you were alone with your thoughts. I stayed under as long as possible, until my lungs started to burn and my chest ached, then broke the surface, gasping.

When I shook the water from my eyes, I saw the raft bobbing three feet away from me. Clinging to the side, grinning at me like the Cheshire cat, was Gwen. I laughed in surprise, pushing a small wave toward her with my hand.

"You beat me!" I said.

"You Starrs are all the same, underestimating my skills just because I learned at the city pool and not in the wilds of the Great White North."

One after the other, we pulled ourselves up on the raft, which shifted under our weight. We lay side by side, wet and sleek, like big white seals come to bathe in the pale light of the moon. It was silent, save for the sloppy sounds of the waves slapping at the raft. It felt good to be shivering slightly in the cool air, muscles tired, lungs stretched, waiting for our breathing to slow down and our heart rates to return to normal.

"It feels like we're the last two people on Earth," Gwen said.

"Mmm," I murmured, not wanting to break the spell.

"I came down here with Bo a few times," she admitted. "I let him win, though. He's a terrible loser."

I smiled, even though I knew she couldn't see me. "Believe me, I know."

I took advantage of Gwen's good mood to apologize. "I'm sorry about Johnny. I just wanted to surprise you. I thought you'd be glad about it."

"I know, Reenie. It was actually a really sweet thing to do, and six weeks ago, I would have been overjoyed." Gwen snorted, then added, "I can't believe you pulled it off, actually. Johnny doesn't do anything he doesn't want to."

"He really wanted to see you," I pointed out.

Gwen squirmed, edging toward the side of the raft. She let her arm dangle over it, her fingers just touching the surface of the lake, which was still and dark, like black glass.

"You must think I'm so stupid, dating a boy like that. But he was so charming and famous . . . I mean, I was dating a rock'n'roll star!"

I did think it was a bad idea, but I couldn't say that out loud, not when she was so fragile. Instead, I said nothing at all, but my silence spoke for me.

"The thing is, my whole life I've always felt like I was two people: Gwendolyn, the good girl, prima ballerina and my mother's prize poodle, and Dolly, the wild girl, the life of the party. I could never seem to mesh the two; people only wanted me to be one or the other. But with Bo, and with you, I was Gwen. I was just me. That probably sounds stupid to you, but it's true."

Gwen put a wet hand over mine. I looked up and found her staring dolefully into my eyes.

"It's not what you think, Reenie. Johnny got it wrong. Your mom has it all wrong. We're not together."

My heart quickened and my stomach clenched. I wasn't sure I wanted to hear this confession.

"I don't understand," I said carefully.

"I mean we weren't dating: we're not a couple. I can understand why everyone thought that, given my reputation and all. But I swear to you, nothing happened."

Relief spread through my body, calming my jitters like calamine on bug bites. I felt like I could breathe normally again. "Then why were you running away?" I asked.

Gwen sighed. "I was going down a bad road, Reenie. I went out with all kinds of boys like Johnny. Boys who aren't much better than rats when push comes to shove. None of them really cared about me, and I started to think that was normal. But then I get here and Bo starts talking to me like I'm a human being . . ." Gwen trailed off, rubbing her hands in her damp hair as if she could shake the words out of her head.

"We weren't in love, at least I don't think we were. We never even kissed. It was weird at first, I mean most boys will try to jam their tongues down your throat any chance they get. But Bo never tried anything with me. We just talked."

"About what?"

"Music, mostly. He played me songs and asked me questions, and he really listened to what I said. My opinion mattered to him. I don't know, Reenie. Nothing happened, but it could have. We were headed that way. I feel like I've lost the love of my life without ever really having him, you know?"

I didn't know, but I pretended to.

"What about Bo?"

Gwen frowned. "What do you mean?"

"Do you think he's in love with you?"

Gwen shook her head, but she didn't look up from the water. "No. At least, I don't think so. He wanted to know all about the city, about the music scene. He listened to my lyrics and put them to music." Gwen looked at me then and held my eyes. "He said he was going to make sure everyone knew my songs."

Suddenly I felt sorry for my brother, who'd fallen under the spell of cool, mysterious Gwen — just like I had. "So you were using him?"

Gwen looked truly stricken. "No! Never! It wasn't like that. If anything, it was like we were using each other. I was his ticket out of here, his connection to the city, and he made me feel like I could do all those things I kept saying I would do."

"So what are you going to do next?"

"Go home, I guess. I keep trying to imagine myself back in the city, but I only get as far as my parents' driveway. All I can think about is the apartment Bo and I talked about getting. We were going to paint an entire wall blue, and Bo was going to draw constellations on it with white chalk."

She smiled faintly, as if she was picturing that wall as we spoke.

"Why?" I asked gently.

Gwen shrugged. "Because we could. We'd be in the city, making music, with no one to tell us what to do. Why shouldn't we put stars on the walls?"

Gwen's voice faltered again, and I waited for more tears to come.

"You can still live in the city and work on your music," I suggested. "You can still paint that wall blue."

"No. Everything's different now. And, as messed up as I am

right now, Bo is worse. He's the one you should be worried about. I was always going back to the city, that was a given. He was really counting on coming with me and now . . ."

"He's stuck here," I finished.

Gwen didn't answer, but she didn't have to. I could tell by the way she looked away across the lake that I was right.

"Maybe he'll go anyway," I said.

Gwen smiled sadly. "Come on, Reenie. Your folks will never let him."

"You don't know that," I protested, thinking of Daddy, and how much he saw, even if he didn't let on. I thought about all the people who had signed up to stay next season, and the others that were bound to call once people got to talking. "Mimi would love a reason to visit the city. I could help Daddy out here. We'd be fine."

I felt chilled, and not just because my skin was still damp. This was a ghost of the conversation I'd had with Daddy out on the lake. I wondered if our words still existed, twisting around the cattails and getting stirred up by the breeze, only to float back to us in bits and pieces.

I rubbed my arms, trying to get rid of the chill.

"Maybe," Gwen said, but I could tell she didn't mean it. She was leaning over the edge of the raft, with her legs submerged up to the knees in the lake. She stared at them, making slow circles in the water, as if they were moving independently from her body, as if they belonged to someone else.

"Did you talk to your mother?" I asked.

"We had a big heart-to-heart," Gwen said. "There was a lot of crying. Her tears, not mine. She feels responsible. A lot of things make sense now, looking back . . . "

Gwen lapsed into silence. I wondered what she meant by that, if there had been clues that she was not Grace's child, but when she didn't offer any explanation I decided to let it go. Maybe it was too painful. When I tried to imagine what it would feel like to have my mother come in and tell me I was adopted after all these years, my brain went completely blank. It was so unbelievable I couldn't even imagine it.

"Are you mad at her?"

Gwen thought for a moment before shaking her head no. "Mostly I feel numb. I feel like I've been through every possible emotion in three days and my body has shut down. Sometimes I'll get so angry, I feel like I could hit someone. But mostly, I'm just here. Not thinking, not doing anything, just numb. I'm sure there's a word for it."

"Shock?" I suggested.

"That sounds about right," Gwen said. "How'd you get so smart?" Then she dipped her hand in the water and pushed a playful wave in my direction. I couldn't help but laugh as it crested and splashed over my thighs.

"So is this what sisters do?" she teased. "Have heart-to-hearts in the middle of the night?"

I smiled. "Sometimes."

"This is nice. I like this. By the way, I never got a chance to tell you how great you were Friday night. You're a natural."

"Thanks," I said. "That feels like a million years ago."

"I know. Back then you were my assistant. Now you're my sister."

"Weird."

"No, not weird. That's the strangest thing about it. In this whole mess, you being my sister feels like the most normal thing in the world."

A New Day

For the first time in days, Gwen showed up for breakfast that morning. I would like to think that it was because of our talk, but, whatever the reason, I was happy to see her participating in the world again. No one made a fuss over her appearance, even Grace, who passed her the milk as if she had been doing it all along. Even so, breakfast was quiet, full of chewing and the sound of cutlery scraping against plates. Mimi was draped over Grace's shoulder, staring at her eggs as if she expected them to grow horns and feet. I didn't think it was possible for the silence to be any deeper, until Bo shuffled in and took a seat next to Daddy.

Gwen looked up and immediately stopped chewing. She swallowed with great effort and pushed her plate away. Her shoulders drooped, and her posture was so like Mimi's that it almost took my breath away. Again, I wondered how I could have missed such a resemblance all summer long.

Scarlett kept glancing back and forth between Gwen and Bo, waiting for something to happen. The atmosphere was so tense all it would take was one wrong word and everything would explode. As I watched the members of my family retreat into themselves and stew in their own thoughts, I remembered what Daddy had said about strengths and decided to act on mine.

"Morning, Bo," I said brightly.

He glared at me and dumped two tablespoons of brown sugar onto his toast, spreading it around with the back of his spoon.

"Want a little toast with your sugar?" I joked.

Bo gave me a thunderous look, but I had lived through more than my fair share of Bo's stormy faces. I would not be put off that easily.

"Maybe you should add another spoonful," I suggested. "You could use a little sweetening this morning."

Bo opened his mouth to speak, but before he could say anything, Gwen piped up.

"I know I could," she said. "So save some for me, would you Bo? I know you're a big rock star and everything, but the little people deserve some sugar, too."

I held my breath as Bo looked at her for the first time. A slow smile crept across his face.

"Well I wouldn't want to keep the prima ballerina from her heart's desire," he said. "She'll throw a tantrum."

I could almost hear the ice breaking and floating away. Scarlett sighed and settled back into her cereal, and Daddy winked at me. Breakfast was still quiet, but it was the kind of calm that follows a storm: peaceful and without danger. The worst was over.

* * *

Grace and Gwen left just after lunch. Mimi went out to say goodbye and the two women stood under the Lookout wrapped in each other's arms for a long time. I watched them from above, in my usual nook in the tree. Grace knew all the shades of Mimi's sadness and the secrets she kept. She probably knew things about Mimi that even Daddy didn't know. They spent months and sometimes years without seeing each other, connected only by a phone wire or the odd letter, and yet when they were together, it was as if all that time disappeared.

I watched until Grace's car turned into a silver streak, flashing in the sun. I wasn't sad; I knew I would see Gwen again. We were sisters, which was exciting, now that I was getting used to it. I'd thought I wanted her to see me as a friend, but a sister was better. We were connected by our shared experiences, but bonded by blood. Our world may have tilted, but some things would never change. Summer would come and go, the leaves would fall, and the geese would return each spring, bearing the sun on their backs.

Bo still had a few years of school left. After that, his sights and his heart were set on the city. That gave Mimi and Daddy some time to warm up to the idea. As for me, I wasn't going anywhere. The city didn't call to me like the loons did.

"Reenie, come down from that tree. There's someone on the phone for you."

I looked down through the solid old branches of the Lookout at Daddy, who was staring up at me with one hand shielding his eyes from the sun.

"Who is it?"

"Someone named Ray," Daddy said.

My heart throbbed so hard I could feel it in my fingertips.

"Coming!" I called. I scrambled down from the Lookout in record time, brushing bits of bark from my hands like dead skin.

"Ray sounds an awful lot like a boy's name," Daddy teased.

I laughed, pausing long enough at the base of the tree for Daddy to wink and ruffle my hair before I ran for the telephone.

At Sandy Shores, the past is all around us: the lodge, built by my grandfather, that always smells sweetly of cedar, even in the dead of winter; the old dock, which is mostly just a plank or two of soft, rotted wood taken over by an army of cattails; and the trees, like the Lookout, which have stood here long before a single Starr set foot on the shores of Sandy Lake. But I can see the future, pushing up through the past like shoots in spring, sweet and green and full of promise. And just like those shoots, I will be here to welcome it when it comes.

Acknowledgements

Reenie Starr walked into my head fully formed one hot summer morning on the back porch of Roxanne Charlebois' Sudbury home. Without the peace and quiet of her home, I may never have heard Reenie calling to me. *Merci*, Roxanne!

Thanks to Sarah Williamson to whom I first described this story on a long drive between Sudbury and Cochrane, and who also kindly opened the door to her dance class so I could observe her teaching ballet to girls about Reenie's age.

Thanks to Kallie George, Rebecca Jess and Nina McCreath for reading an early section that eventually went on to score me a much needed OAC grant.

Thank you to the Ontario Arts Council for their generous financial support in the form of a Writer's Works in Progress Grant, which allowed me the time and freedom to focus on Reenie's world.

Thanks to Sally Harding, Jennifer MacKinnon, Diane Kerner, Denise Anderson, and Nikole Kritikos for always having my back and for believing in Sandy Shores as much as I did, and to Aldo Fierro, who has now created four amazing covers for me, including that dreamy, summery master-piece on the front of this book.

Thanks to my sisters in writing, Kallie George and Grace O'Connell, and my urban family, Rob Kempson and Rebecca Jess.

Although this is a work of fiction, I have been influenced by the summer vacations my family took and by the music and culture of the 1960s, which my parents loved. They have instilled that same love in me.

One final thank you to my parents, Joanne and Craig VanSickle, who gave me an ideal childhood on which I can build other worlds and dreams.

About Vikki

Vikki VanSickle grew up in Woodstock, Ontario and now lives in Toronto with her two wonderful roommates and a cat who loves nothing more than to help her revise.

She is the author of three books about Clarissa Delaney and her loyal friend Benji, and is an active member of the children's literature community.

She also reviews children's books for several publications and on her blog. When she is not writing and reviewing, Vikki works as a children's marketing specialist and sees as much musical theatre as she can.

Other books by Vikki VanSickle:
Words That Start With B
Love Is a Four-Letter Word
Days That End in Y